"Let's see what [...]
Mitchell Martins [...]
social media, too."

She pulled up the site and then gasped in obvious horror and pulled her fingers off the keyboard. "That's Max." Her voice trembled as her face paled.

Troy looked at the photo of the scruffy dark-haired man and then gazed back at Eliza. "Max who?" he asked in confusion.

"Max... He was the man who came here earlier and pretended to be from the power company."

The man had pretended to be an electrical technician to get into the house. Why? They had to figure out what the hell was going on. All of a sudden he didn't smell Eliza's enchanting scent or feel the warmth of her body close to his.

All he felt at the moment was a tight twist of his gut as a dark cloud of danger descended over her.

DESPERATE INTENTIONS

New York Times Bestselling Author
CARLA CASSIDY

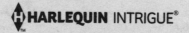 HARLEQUIN INTRIGUE®

Recycling programs
for this product may
not exist in your area.

ISBN-13: 978-1-335-60417-0

Desperate Intentions

Printed in U.S.A.

Carla Cassidy is an award-winning, *New York Times* bestselling author who has written more than 120 novels for Harlequin. In 1995, she won Best Silhouette Romance from *RT Book Reviews* for *Anything for Danny*. In 1998, she won a Career Achievement Award for Best Innovative Series from *RT Book Reviews*. Carla believes the only thing better than curling up with a good book to read is sitting down at the computer with a good story to write.

Books by Carla Cassidy

Harlequin Intrigue

Scene of the Crime

Scene of the Crime: Bridgewater, Texas
Scene of the Crime: Bachelor Moon
Scene of the Crime: Widow Creek
Scene of the Crime: Mystic Lake
Scene of the Crime: Black Creek
Scene of the Crime: Deadman's Bluff
Scene of the Crime: Return to Bachelor Moon
Scene of the Crime: Return to Mystic Lake
Scene of the Crime: Baton Rouge
Scene of the Crime: Killer Cove
Scene of the Crime: Who Killed Shelly Sinclair?
Scene of the Crime: Means and Motive

Desperate Strangers
Desperate Intentions

Visit the Author Profile page at Harlequin.com.

CAST OF CHARACTERS

Eliza Burke—Single mother of two children who doesn't realize the danger she's in.

Troy Anderson—Had the murder of his daughter turned him into a monster?

Leon Decker—A man with a grudge who has promised to destroy Eliza's life.

Max Sampson—Was he just an odd utility worker or somebody far more dangerous?

Frank Malone—Had the dead mobster left Eliza a haunted house? Or was there something more dangerous than ghosts in the house?

Prologue

He dug the grave deep...and deeper still, not wanting anyone to ever find it. The moonlight overhead was bright, but at one o'clock in the morning in his own backyard he wasn't too worried about anyone seeing him.

Troy Anderson leaned against the shovel handle and swiped the sweat that threatened to drip into his eyes. Even though it was the middle of the night, the heat was relentless. August in Kansas City always brought high temperatures and thick humidity.

He stared down into the deep hole he had dug, his emotions curiously numb. The man was dead, setting into motion a plot to murder another man...a man whose death Troy had dreamed about and had yearned for, for a thousand nights.

This was what he'd wanted for three long years. So why didn't a delirious happiness fill him? Why didn't a wild anticipation thrum inside him? The man who had destroyed his life and stolen his happiness now had an expiration date, and all that Troy felt was numb.

He swiped his forehead once again and got back to shoveling the hard dirt. His T-shirt clung to his chest and the latex gloves he wore smothered the skin of his hands. He couldn't wait to get them off.

When he had the hole dug deep enough for his satisfaction, he turned and grabbed the white plastic grocer's bag on the ground next to him. He pulled out the gun inside and held it for several long minutes in his hand.

It was the weapon he was supposed to use on this night to kill a man named Steven Winthrop. Troy had never met Winthrop, but he knew the man was responsible for the rape and murder of a woman who had just been doing her job in showing a home to a prospective buyer. Winthrop had beat the system and walked away a free man, even though everyone had known he was guilty.

Troy had tossed and turned the night before with the knowledge that he intended to take a man's life. He intended to commit cold-blooded murder. But it was the only path to the vigilante justice he needed… that he wanted so badly.

He'd awakened that morning with murder in mind only to open the daily newspaper and discover that

Steven Winthrop had been murdered the night before. According to the report, the man's throat had been sliced open in his bedroom.

So Troy would not be required to commit murder for the plan to continue. He had no idea who had owned or used this particular gun before it had appeared in his mailbox with instructions as to the date and time to kill Winthrop. He had no idea how many other murders the gun might be tied to. The serial numbers had been scratched off, but he knew there were now ways and technologies to retrieve the number. He had to get rid of it, and this was the only way he knew how. He dropped the gun into the hole and then shoveled dirt over the top.

He buried the weapon and when he was finished, once again he leaned on the shovel and fought against a bone-deep weariness. He needed to take a long shower and then go to bed. He needed the sweet oblivion of sleep to quiet the demons in his head.

He straightened up and his gaze swept to his neighbor's big three-story house. He froze. Silhouetted in a second-floor window was somebody. Somebody watching him...somebody who had seen him bury the gun.

Chapter One

"Mommy, I want to wear my pink shoes but I can't find them," Katie called from her upstairs bedroom.

"The school bus is going to be here in five minutes. I don't care what color shoes you wear, but you must have shoes on both feet." Eliza Burke drew in a deep breath to find patience.

Every morning for the past week since school had started, it was the same chaotic scramble to get both her children on separate school buses. Her daughter, Katie, went to second grade at one school, and her son, Sammy, went on a little yellow bus to the Kansas City school for the blind.

"Katie," she called up the stairs. "We have to go." She turned to Sammy, who sat at the kitchen table. "I swear, your sister is going to make me old before my time."

Sammy giggled. "But we still love her."

"Yes, we still love her," Eliza agreed.

"I'm coming," Katie called. Her footsteps rang out as she came down the stairs. She appeared in the kitchen, a blue shoe on one foot and a pink one on the other. "Shoes on both feet," she proclaimed proudly. Eliza sighed.

"Grab your lunch bags and let's head to the bus stop," she said. "We don't want to miss the buses."

Together the three of them left the house. Sammy held her arm more for comfort than for guidance. He had astounded her with his quick acclimation to the new house and neighborhood.

An edge of grief swept through her as his hand warmed her forearm. Sammy had the most beautiful blue eyes with stunning dark lashes, but something had gone wrong and he'd been born without sight. Still, he was smart as a whip and a very happy child.

Katie was her seven-year-old drama queen. She loved fashion and all things with bling. She also loved her younger brother with a fierce intensity. There was only one year between the two and they were very close.

They had just reached the bus stop a block away from the house when Katie's bus rumbled to a halt before them. With kisses given, she disappeared up the stairs and onto the bus.

Minutes later Sammy was gone as well and Eliza started the walk back home. Home. The unexpected gift of the huge three-story house had been a happy, shocking surprise that had gotten them out of the crummy apartment building where they had been living.

It had been left to her by her ex-husband's grandfather, a man Eliza had barely known. But it was paid off, and a month ago she and the children had moved in.

She entered the house and went directly to the kitchen to check on the slow cooker meal she'd started an hour earlier. She could already smell the chicken and tomatoes cooking.

She then went into the room that was now her office. It was an odd-shaped room, as many of them were in the big home. This one was a disproportional octagon.

She grabbed a hair tie and pulled her hair up into a messy ponytail atop her head, and then sat at the desk. When Sammy was two years old her husband, Blake, had left her…had left them.

She'd desperately needed a job and yet also needed to be home to take care of a blind child. That was when she'd begun her web design business, and thankfully it had flourished and grown to the point she was able to keep up with the bills and see that her children were well-fed and clothed.

Of course moving into this house where there

was no rent or mortgage was going to help out tremendously. Not only did she need to start saving for college for the kids, she also wanted to get Sammy a guide dog when he turned sixteen. For the first time since Blake had walked out on them she had the real hope that those things would happen.

However, nothing was going to happen if she didn't get down to work right now. Mentally shoving her thoughts of her children away, she opened up her email. Reading her email had become an unpleasant task since Leon Whitaker had entered her life. Today was no different. There were three emails and two texts from the man threatening to destroy her life.

She sighed, wondering when Leon would finally move on and leave her alone. She deleted them, and at the same time her doorbell rang. She jumped up and hurried to answer.

She opened the door to find her smoking-hot next-door neighbor standing on the porch. She hadn't officially met him yet, but had watched him mowing his lawn on more than one occasion, his broad bare back gleaming in the sunshine.

"Hi." He smiled, showing teeth that were straight and white. He set down the large flowering plant he held in one arm. "I thought it was about time I came over to officially introduce myself and welcome you to the neighborhood. I'm Troy Anderson."

"Hi, I'm Eliza… Eliza Burke." She looked down at the plant. "It's gorgeous." Huge flowers in a beautiful shade of deep pink adorned the sturdy green stalks. She fought the impulse to reach up and do something with her messy hair.

"It's a peony. I thought it might look nice right there next to your porch." He pointed to a bare spot and then looked at her expectantly.

"What a nice thought. Uh, would you like to sit and have a cup of coffee?" She gestured to the porch swing. It would be nice to get to know her neighbor, although it would be much more comfortable if he weren't so darned good-looking. A wild flutter of butterflies had taken wing in her chest the moment he'd first smiled at her.

"I'd love a cup of coffee," he replied. He stepped past her, trailing the scent of sunshine and an attractive woodsy cologne on his way to the swing.

"Uh, I'll be right back." She stepped back inside and locked the door behind her. She never lost track of the fact that she was a woman living here only with her two small children.

While Troy appeared to be a decent, law-abiding citizen, she didn't feel comfortable enough to invite him inside, at least not yet. Still, it had been very nice of him to come over and bring the plant.

Darn, she should have asked him if he used cream

or sugar in his coffee. She placed a pod in the coffee machine and waited for it to whoosh out Colombian caffeine into the mug.

When it was finished she hurried back outside. "I didn't think to ask you if you wanted anything in your coffee."

"Black is fine," he assured her as he took the cup from her. She sank down in a nearby wicker chair.

"So, I've seen some children in your backyard," he said.

"Yes, Sammy and Katie." She couldn't help the smile that curved her lips as she thought of her children. "Katie is seven and Sammy is six."

"And Mr. Burke?" His eyes were an intense blue as they held her gaze.

"There is no Mr. Burke," she replied, deciding to be honest. Thoughts of Blake always made her angry and sad at the same time. "What about you? Is there a Mrs. Anderson?"

"No, I'm divorced. No wife and no children." A darkness crept into his eyes. It was there only a moment and then vanquished by another one of his heart-stopping smiles. "So, Ms. Eliza Burke, what do you do for a living? the nosy neighbor asked." He raised his cup to his lips and took a sip.

"I have my own web design business," she said. "And I assume you're Troy Anderson as in Anderson

Lawn and Landscaping. I've seen your truck parked in front of your house."

The butterflies continued to fly. What on earth was wrong with her? She hadn't had that kind of a reaction to a man for years.

"That's me," he replied. "Maybe we can trade services. I'll take care of your lawn and you can update my website."

"I'm sure we can work something out." Actually she hadn't thought about the lawn, since right now everything was summer brown and needed no tending.

"And I'll be glad to plant the peony for you."

"That's too kind of you," she protested.

"Nonsense, I brought it, so I'll plant it. I'll get it taken care of sometime tomorrow." He took another sip of the coffee. "I couldn't help but notice when you opened your door that something in there smells wonderful," he said.

"I've got chicken cacciatore in the Crock-Pot."

"Oh, that's one of my favorite dishes." Once again he appeared to be looking at her in expectation.

"If you'd like to join us this evening we usually sit down to eat around five." The words were out of her mouth before she realized she was going to speak them.

"That sounds great. I'd love to join you." He

took another drink of his coffee and then stood and walked toward her to hand her the cup. "I should get going, but I look forward to seeing you again this evening, Eliza. Thanks so much for the coffee and the invitation."

She stood and watched him until he disappeared into his house. Only then did she turn and go back inside. She returned to her desk and frowned thoughtfully. The short conversation had been rather strained and she felt strangely manipulated into the dinner invitation…and strangely excited at the same time.

TROY HEADED BACK to his house, his mind working overtime to process what he'd just learned. Eliza Burke was definitely a stunner. Her dark hair pulled up in the ponytail had showcased beautiful gray eyes and prominent cheekbones.

But he hadn't gone over there to check out the physical attributes of the new neighbor. He needed to find out who had stood in the upstairs window and watched him bury the gun. He now knew she didn't have a husband, but was another adult living with her? Was there somebody else besides her and the two children in the house? Somebody who had seen what he had done?

Worming his way into a dinner invitation had been absolutely perfect. Hopefully he'd know tonight what had been seen and by whom. In the meantime he had other concerns whirling around in his head.

Somebody had killed Steven Winthrop and that meant somebody was playing by their own set of rules. He knew Nick Simon had encountered a similar problem and even though it was against the terms they had all set up among themselves, Troy wanted to meet with Nick.

He pulled his cell phone from his pocket and punched in Nick's phone number. Nick answered on the second ring. "Nick, it's Troy."

There was a long pause and Troy knew he was probably the last man on earth Nick wanted to hear from right now. "Hey," Nick finally replied, his voice obviously strained.

"I want to meet with you," Troy said.

Again a long pause followed. "Do you think it's really necessary?"

"I think it is," Troy replied. "Please, Nick."

A deep sigh filled the line. "When?"

"Now, if possible."

"I'll meet you in thirty minutes at the usual place," Nick said, and then hung up.

Five minutes later Troy was in his work truck and headed to the old abandoned baseball field where the six men had plotted a murder scheme that would assure each of them both vengeance and the justice that had been denied.

As he approached his destination, tension bunched his shoulders and he gripped the steering wheel more tightly. He couldn't come here without thinking of Annie, and thoughts of her always brought forth a deep grief, a hollow emptiness and also a rage tempered only a little bit by the passing of time.

Knee-high weeds greeted him as he stepped out of the truck. Nature was in the process of taking back the land that had once been filled with a ball field and little baseball players.

The wooden bleachers in the distance leaned to one side, broken and bleached almost white from the summer sun. A snack shed was spray-painted with a variety of words in different colors. Even that paint had faded, attesting to the forgotten nature of the property.

He walked toward the thick stand of trees in the distance. It was there next to a fallen tree that a plot for murder had been hatched among six grieving, angry men.

They had met two years ago at a group meeting for survivors. All six of them had a couple of things in common. The first was that the perpetrators who had committed horrendous crimes against their loved ones had walked away free men due to glitches in their cases. The second thing they all had in common was a killing rage and a desperate and hungry need for justice.

They had set up a plan for each of them to kill another man's perpetrator. They each would be killing a man who had absolutely nothing to do with them, hopefully assuring that they all stayed under law enforcement's scrutiny.

Troy now headed into the woods. Even in the shade it was hot, and insects buzzed angrily as if to protest Troy's presence in their domain. He didn't want to be here. He didn't want to think about the crime that had brought him here. But it concerned him that one of the six was apparently acting alone, and that hadn't been the plan.

He sat on the fallen log to wait for Nick and tried to keep his mind empty, but it was impossible. Surprisingly it wasn't thoughts of murder, but rather thoughts of his neighbor Eliza Burke that intruded in his head.

It had been a long time since Troy had really noticed any woman. After his wife had walked out on him three years before, he'd had no interest in any kind of a relationship.

However, Eliza Burke had stirred him on a level he'd thought was long dead. She'd sparked something inside him he hadn't felt for a very long time.

Not that anything would come of it. He wouldn't allow anything to come of it even if she was interested in him.

He just wanted to know who in her house might have seen him last night. He'd join her for dinner and see if he got the answer. Once that question was answered, he would be done with her.

Before he had time to really process anything more, Nick appeared. The tall, dark-haired man wore a deep frown. "What's up?" He leaned against a nearby tree as if not wanting to get too close to Troy.

"I was supposed to kill Winthrop last night, but somebody got to him before me."

Nick grimaced. "Just like what happened to me."

"Somebody has gone rogue and it's got me worried."

"Look, I don't want anything to do with this," Nick protested. "I've moved on. I'm in love with a wonderful woman and we're planning a wedding."

"I know you don't want to be involved in this, but you are," Troy replied evenly. "Doesn't it bother you that one of us is acting alone? Do you have any idea who it might be?"

Nick frowned again. "Adam is the one who planned all this. Maybe he just decided to take things into his own hands."

Adam Kincaid was one of the six men who had

taken the lead and was in charge of the logistics of the plan. His wife had been murdered at a drive-through ATM where she had just withdrawn two hundred dollars. A drug-addicted man had yanked her out of the car and had stabbed her to death to get the cash. The case had ended in a hung jury and the prosecutor had decided not to retry the case.

"If that's true, then you know what that makes all of the rest of us? Liabilities," Troy said.

Nick raised an eyebrow. "Do you really think he'd come after one of us?"

Troy released a deep sigh. "I don't know what to think. I just wanted you to know that somebody isn't playing by the rules we all set up, although I have to admit I was kind of relieved to wake up yesterday morning and realize I didn't have to kill a man."

"Yeah, I felt the same way when my target was already dead when I went to his house to kill him." Nick's frown appeared once again and his eyes darkened. "I've got to tell you, man, that was a bad scene. Whoever killed Brian McDowell enjoyed it. His throat was slit, and that takes a special kind of killer. There was also a carving in his forehead. It looked like a *V*."

Tension once again tugged at Troy's shoulders. "*V* for vengeance? For vigilante?"

"Could be either, or maybe it was just a coincidence that it looked like a *V*. But who does that? Who carves up a man's forehead after slitting his throat?"

"Hell if I know. So, what do we do about it?"

"Nothing. I told all of you before that I'm out of it. I feel like I made a pact with the devil when I got involved in this crazy scheme," Nick replied.

Troy studied him for a long moment. "How did you feel this morning when you woke up and read that the man who raped and killed your wife was dead?"

"Nothing," Nick replied. "I felt nothing. My wife was still dead and Winthrop's murder didn't change that. I'm building a new life for myself and that's all that matters to me now." He straightened from the tree trunk. "I hope nothing more comes of this, Troy, but in any case, please lose my number forever."

Nick turned and left the small clearing. Troy remained on the log, trying to figure out what in the hell he had hoped to accomplish by meeting with Nick. Maybe he'd just needed somebody else to know.

Troy didn't want to think about the pact anymore. He knew somebody was going to kill Dwight Weatherby. Troy definitely wanted that man dead, and he wasn't about to do a damned thing to stop that from happening.

And that made him a bad man.

Chapter Two

Nervous energy filled Eliza as she set the table for the evening meal with an extra plate. Would he show up for dinner? On the off chance he would she'd changed into a nicer pair of black skinny jeans and a lavender blouse that she knew complemented her gray eyes. She'd also let her hair down and it now fell around her shoulders in soft waves.

She was a fool to be going to so much trouble, she'd thought as she'd applied a little more mascara and then a dash of pink lip gloss.

It wasn't like she was looking for romance. When Blake had left her she'd pretty much put that part of herself away forever. Besides, she was hardly an attractive package for any man to take on, considering the fact that she had two young children and one of them was blind.

Tonight wasn't about romance. It was about learning a little bit about the man who was her neighbor.

She didn't know about him, but she intended to be in this house for a very long time. Building good neighbor relationships couldn't be a bad thing.

"Mom, come and look what Sammy found," Katie called from the living room.

Eliza pulled garlic bread out of the oven and then went to check on the children. "What did you find, Sammy?" she asked.

He ran his fingers along the white wainscoting and a panel popped open, revealing a space big enough for the two of them to stand in. "It's a secret hiding spot," he said.

"Would you look at that," Eliza said in amazement, although this wasn't the first surprise the house had given up. Two weeks after moving in, Sammy had found a hidden stairway that went from Katie's room down to the kitchen pantry.

"That is a great hiding place," she said. She stepped inside to make sure there was nothing dangerous in the space. "It could be your very own secret hideaway. But right now I want you two to wash your hands and faces for dinner. It's possible we might have a visitor."

"A visitor?" Katie's face lit up. "Who is it? Ms. Lucy?"

"Not Ms. Lucy. Our neighbor might come to eat with us. Now go get cleaned up. Dinner is going to be on the table in about three minutes." As the two headed for the bathroom, Eliza returned to the kitchen.

The clock on the oven read seven minutes until five. It was very possible he wouldn't show up at all and that was okay with her. The whole thing had been rather strange to begin with.

The food was on the table and the children had just been seated when the doorbell rang. "Wait here, I'll be right back," she said, and tried to ignore the bolt of anticipation that leaped into the pit of her stomach.

He stood on the front porch with his sexy smile and the sun gleaming on his slightly shaggy dark hair. His jeans hugged his slender hips and emphasized his broad chest beneath a light blue cotton shirt. "I hope I'm not too late. I got held up at work." He thrust a bottle of red wine toward her.

"Actually, you're just in time," she replied, and took the wine from him. "You didn't have to do that," she added as she gestured him inside. She led him into the kitchen. "Sammy and Katie, this is our neighbor, Mr. Anderson."

"I know you. You buried treasure in your backyard in the middle of the night last night," Katie said with a wide smile. "I love treasure."

He rocked back on his heels and Eliza could swear

his handsome face paled. Then he laughed. "Oh, honey, that was no treasure. Unfortunately I found a dead cat in my yard and I had to bury it."

"And what were you doing up in the middle of the night, young lady?" Eliza asked her daughter.

"I woked up and went into Sammy's room 'cause I thought he might have a nightmare," Katie said. She batted long dark lashes. "You know I don't want Sammy to ever get scared."

Eliza turned to her guest. "Please, have a seat, Troy." She gestured to the chair at the head of the table.

They began to fill their plates. "Why did the cat die?" Katie asked once everyone had been served.

"I don't know," Troy replied.

"Chicken at six, bread at three and salad at nine," Eliza murmured softly to Sammy.

Troy looked at Sammy and then gazed at Eliza. She knew at that moment he'd realized Sammy was blind. He cleared his throat and then cast her a smile that warmed her from head to toe.

"My daddy died," Katie said. "So my daddy and that cat are both in heaven together."

"Did your dad like cats?" Troy asked.

Katie looked at Eliza. "Did he, Mom?"

"I'm sure he did," Eliza replied. She never wanted her children to know how much she'd come to hate their father during the time before he'd walked out on them. He had died less than a year later in a motorcycle accident in Florida.

"So, tell me about your landscaping business," she said to Troy in an effort to engage him and change the subject.

"It started with just me, a truck and a lawn mower," he said. "I've always enjoyed yard work, and I now have ten trucks and a crew of men and women who work for me."

"Wow, that's impressive."

"I've been lucky in scoring a lot of big commercial jobs. By the way, this chicken is delicious."

"Thank you," she replied.

"Mom is a great cook," Sammy said.

"And she's pretty. Don't you think she's very pretty, Mr. Anderson?" Katie asked with a winsome smile.

"Katie," Eliza said with a blush creeping warmth into her cheeks.

Troy laughed. "Yes, Katie, your mother is very pretty."

The rest of the meal passed with the children chattering about their schools and their favorite playtime activities. Eliza was acutely aware of Troy's presence, far too aware since he was just a neighbor who had joined them for a meal.

She was also particularly proud of her children, who displayed good manners throughout the meal.

"Is your house as crazy as this one?" Sammy asked.

"What do you mean by crazy?" Troy asked.

"I found a secret hidey-hole in the living room and a secret stairway in Katie's bedroom that comes down into the kitchen pantry," he replied.

Troy looked at Eliza. "It's true," she said. "The house does appear to have a lot of secrets."

"I wanna find some buried treasure," Katie piped up. "I love treasure, 'specially if it sparkles."

Eliza and Troy laughed. "Is that why you bought the house? To look for buried treasure?"

She laughed again. "Not hardly, and we didn't buy the house, we inherited it. It was left to us by my late husband's grandfather when he passed away a couple of months ago. I have to admit it was quite a surprise."

"I wondered why a for-sale sign didn't go up when Frank passed away," Troy replied.

By that time everyone had finished eating and the children asked to be excused to go watch television. "I insist on helping with the cleanup," Troy said.

"And I insist you don't," she replied. "Why don't I make you a cup of coffee and you can sit and talk to me while I handle the cleanup?"

"Okay, if you insist," he replied easily.

Minutes later with a cup of coffee before him, Troy told her a little bit more about his business. His father had bought him his first lawn mower when he was ten years old and had encouraged him to become a little entrepreneur.

"I never thought about doing anything else," he said. "I love working outside and helping people transform their landscaping from something ugly into something beautiful."

"It's always nice to love what you do," she replied.

"I take it you love what you do." He eyed her over the rim of the coffee cup.

"Most of the time, unless I get a crazy client. I've got a man now who is sending me dozens of nasty texts and emails a day over a project."

His eyes widened. "Why?"

She put the leftover chicken in the refrigerator and then turned to face him. "I agreed to build a web page for him and then realized halfway into it that it was going to be a pornographic site, and so I backed out of the deal. I refunded the initial money he gave to me and thought that would be the end of it, but he's been harassing me for weeks now."

"Have you called the police to report him?" Troy asked.

"Oh no, it hasn't risen to that kind of a level. It's just a nuisance."

"I know it's just you and the kids here. If anything does ever get out of hand with him just remember I'm right next door."

"Thank you, I appreciate that. You don't happen to know a good exterminator, do you? I think we might have a mouse problem. The kids and I are hearing some rustling behind the walls at night."

"Actually, I do. Mike the Mighty Mouseman."

She grinned. "Is that for real?"

He laughed and shook his head. "It's for real. He's a friend of mine. We went to school together and have remained good friends. Do you want me to give you his number?"

"Please." She pulled her cell phone out of her pocket and punched in the number he rattled off.

"Let me give you my number, too," he said. He pulled out his cell phone. "And I'd like yours, if that's okay. It's always good to have a neighbor's phone number."

They exchanged phone numbers and he returned

to drinking his coffee. "You should like the neighborhood. It's a quiet one."

"After living in a noisy apartment complex, quiet is good," she replied.

"Most of the people are older and have lived here for years. I haven't met many, but the ones I have met have been very nice."

"That's good to know," she replied. "I guess the house on the other side of me is empty. I noticed a moving van there last week and then a for-sale sign in front of it the other day."

He nodded. "The Fosters. They were an older couple. They decided the house was too big for the two of them."

"They are big houses," she replied. "I don't know what to do with half the space I have here."

"I'm using a couple of rooms upstairs strictly for storage." He finished the last of his coffee and then rose from the table. "I guess I'd better get out of your hair. This has been very pleasant. Thank you for inviting me."

"Thank you for coming," she replied. "It's always nice to know your neighbors." Together they walked to the front door. It had been pleasant. It had been a long time since she'd had an evening of adult conversation, and it hadn't hurt that he was so darned easy to look at.

Two hours later she sat on the edge of Katie's bed to tuck her in for the night. "No sneaking into your brother's room in the middle of the night," she said, and swiped a strand of long dark hair away from Katie's face.

"But what if I wake up in the middle of the night and I think maybe he's having a nightmare?" Katie's gray eyes darkened. "I don't ever want Sammy to be scared."

"And I appreciate you looking after Sammy so well. But your brother will call to me if he has a nightmare and gets scared," Eliza said, "and all princesses need to stay in bed and get their rest through the night."

"And I *am* a princess," Katie replied firmly.

"Absolutely, you're my little special princess." Eliza leaned over and kissed her daughter on the cheek. "Good night, sweetheart."

"Night, Mommy."

Eliza rose from the bed and turned out the overhead light, then walked across the hall into Sammy's bedroom. His twin bed was pushed against one wall and his dresser was against another. There was nothing on the floor to impede him in his world of darkness.

He knew how many steps to the bathroom and how many to the top of the stairs. She had wanted to put his bedroom downstairs, but he'd insisted he wanted to be up here where his sister's room was. He was such an amazing little guy, and she was blessed to be his mother.

Sammy never complained about any nightmares. Eliza had a feeling Katie sometimes had bad dreams and went into her brother's bedroom for comfort.

She sat on the edge of his bed and he smiled. "Are you ready for sweet dreams?" she asked.

"As long as the mice stay quiet."

"We're going to take care of those noisy, pesky mice very soon," she replied. "In the meantime I want you to have sweet dreams and I'll see you in the morning. It's Saturday so you can sleep in if you want."

"I think I might want to," he replied.

She kissed him and then with final good-nights said, she left his room and headed for her own.

This big old house still didn't feel like home to her, but it would just take more time. At least Sammy had adapted easily, and initially that had been her biggest concern. As she changed into her nightgown, her thoughts filled with Troy Anderson.

Lordy, but the man was hot and he'd seemed to be genuinely nice. He'd been especially good with Sammy, not talking to him like he was stupid or raising his voice like Sammy was deaf as well as blind.

She got into bed and shut off her light. It had been nice to have a man to share a meal and pleasant conversation. Still, it didn't matter whether he had given her dancing butterflies or not. She'd felt those same kind of dancing butterflies when she'd first met Blake and that had certainly ended badly.

She released a deep sigh and hoped the mice would stay silent tonight.

TROY PARKED HIS work truck in the driveway and released a weary sigh. Even though it was just a little after three, it had been a long day.

Two of his men hadn't shown up for work that morning. Thankfully the jobs had been residential mows and trimming, so Troy had taken care of them himself. But this was the third time the two had missed an early Saturday morning job and now he needed to decide if they needed to be let go.

Troy always hated firing anyone, but he did expect his employees to be dependable. Thankfully the men were young and unmarried, so at least Troy didn't have to worry about them having families they were supporting.

He got out of his truck and glanced next door. Instantly a bit of adrenaline filled him as he thought of Eliza. There was no question he found her intensely physically attractive. He'd also found her charming and nice, but he hadn't missed a few times when her beautiful gray eyes darkened with emotions that had intrigued him. He was also impressed by her strength. It must be tough to be a single mother of two young kids, especially with one of them being blind.

He'd said he'd plant the peony bush, and he was vaguely surprised to realize the idea of seeing Eliza again today swept a pleasant warmth through him. He should plant it right now before he took a shower and cleaned up. But first what he wanted to do before anything else was go inside and get a tall glass of something cold to drink.

He walked into his hallway of gleaming wood floors. He'd bought the big three-story house a year and a half ago. It had needed a ton of work, but he'd been looking for a new start and the remodeling had been a project he'd desperately needed to take his mind away from the torment of his past.

He'd stripped floors and painted walls. He'd updated the bathrooms and had all the windows replaced. He'd considered every dollar he spent and all his sweat and hard work a good investment. And the work had definitely kept him from losing his mind.

The kitchen had been updated with all the bells and whistles. As he headed toward the refrigerator he glanced out the back window…and froze.

The two kids, Katie and Sammy, were in his yard

and standing over the place where he'd buried the gun. What the hell? What were they doing in his yard, in that place? Thirst forgotten, he ran toward the back door.

He unlocked it and flung it open, and at the same time Eliza appeared, running toward her children. "Katie! Sammy! What on earth are you doing over here?" She flashed him an apologetic glance and then glared at her children once again. "You both know the rules. You are never, ever to leave the house without telling me. And you especially should not be over here in Mr. Anderson's yard. What were the two of you thinking?"

"We just wanted to have a funeral for the dead cat," Katie said, her lower lip trembling ominously as she looked first at her mother and then at Troy.

"We're sorry, Mommy," Sammy said. "We thought it would be good to have a cat funeral."

For the first time Troy realized Katie was wearing what appeared to be a black dress that belonged to her mother and Sammy wore some kind of a black curtain draped over his shoulders. Katie held a small bouquet of plastic flowers and Sammy held a cardboard sign that read RIP Cat.

Jeez, the kids wanted to have a funeral for the cat that didn't exist. What damned can of worms had he opened with his lie about the cat? He frowned thoughtfully. Maybe by allowing them to do this, they'd forget they saw him bury anything out here.

"It's all right," Troy said to Eliza. "Every dead cat should have a funeral."

Eliza looked charmingly flustered. Her cheeks were flushed as she blew a strand of hair off her face. The grateful look she gave him warmed him.

"Okay, you can have a funeral, but when we get home there are going to be consequences for you breaking the rules," she said to her children. "And you can thank Mr. Anderson for not chasing you out of his yard with a broom."

"Thank you, Mr. Anderson," Katie said with a sweet smile that suddenly reminded him of Annie.

For a brief moment a deep, rich pain ripped through his very soul. Thankfully at that moment Katie instructed them all to close their eyes. He squeezed his eyelids closed and tried to will away the memories that attempted to assault him.

He'd spent the last three years of his life trying not to remember, because remembering had the power to cast him to his knees in the very depths of hell. He drew several long, deep breaths and managed to snap himself out of the past.

"We come together to say goodbye to Cat," Katie began.

"We decided that Cat was a good name since we

didn't know his real name," Sammy added. "Mr. Anderson, was Cat a boy or a girl?"

"A boy," Troy replied.

"We all pray for boy Cat to go straight to heaven where the trees are made of catnip and cats are happy all the time," Katie said. "We can open our eyes now."

He opened to see Katie bending down and placing the little flower bouquet on the ground. "Ashes to ashes, dust to dust. I don't know what that means but they always say it at funerals," Katie said. She turned toward her brother and took the makeshift cardboard tombstone from him. "We don't know why people write *RIP* on tombstones, but we've seen it in movies so we wrote *RIP Cat*."

"It stands for *rest in peace*. You know, that sign is going to get all wet when it rains and it won't take much time for the writing to fade. Why don't I buy a nice birdbath to put here?" Troy said. "Cats like birds."

"Oh, that would be wonderful," Katie exclaimed, and jumped up and down with excitement.

"Troy, you don't have to do that," Eliza protested.

"It's all right," he assured her. "I've been wanting a birdbath out here anyway." And he hoped that placing a birdbath there would halt any further interest in the "dead cat."

"That's the end of the funeral," Sammy said.

"And the beginning of your consequences." Eliza pointed toward her house. "I want you two to march yourselves right back home and go to your rooms. We'll discuss your punishment when I get back inside."

When the children were out of earshot she turned to look at Troy. "I'm so sorry. I promise you they have never done anything like this before."

"It's okay. Have they been to a lot of funerals?" he asked.

"Not a one, which makes me question what they've been watching on television when I'm not paying attention. Anyway, I apologize once again and I certainly don't expect you to go out and buy a birdbath."

"Actually, they just prodded me to do something I'd been thinking about doing for some time." She looked so pretty with the sunshine playing in the dark strands of her hair and her eyes the gray of a dove's wing. Did her eyes darken to a smoky gray when she was in the throes of passion?

The totally inappropriate thought shocked him and he mentally shook himself. "If it's okay with you I thought I'd grab my shovel and plant that peony." Maybe a little physical activity would stop any more lustful thoughts he entertained about his pretty neighbor.

"That would be wonderful. In the meantime I need to get back inside to hand out punishments," she replied.

"Don't be too hard on them."

She flashed him a brilliant smile that warmed him more than the summer sun overhead. "I'm never too hard on them. I like to think I'm fair."

"Fair is always good. I'll be in your front yard in just a few minutes."

He watched her as she walked back toward her house, unable to help but notice the slight sway of her shapely hips. Damn, but she was one fine-looking woman.

As she disappeared from view he frowned and headed back into his house. In the kitchen, he fixed himself a tall glass of lemonade and then after drinking it headed to the garage for a shovel.

His feelings toward Eliza disturbed him. Throughout nine years of marriage he'd never had lustful thoughts for any woman except his wife. Since Sherry had walked out on him almost three years before, he'd never had any inappropriate thoughts about another woman.

So why now? And why Eliza? He certainly wasn't looking for any kind of a relationship, especially with a woman who had children. All he'd wanted to do was find out who, in her house, had seen him bury the gun. He had his answer and so that should be the end of things.

But there was a part of him that didn't want it to be the end of things. He needed to ignore that part... as soon as he planted the bush. He needed to keep his distance from his lovely, single neighbor.

He grabbed his shovel and then headed across the yard to her front porch, where the plant remained where he had left it the day before.

There had been no rain for the past two weeks and the ground was hard as a rock. What he needed was a garden hose, not only to soften the dirt but also to water the bush once it had been placed in the ground.

Looking around, he spied a faucet to connect one, but none was in sight. He knocked lightly on the front door. "Do you have a water hose?" he asked when she answered.

She frowned, a delicate gesture that didn't detract from her overall loveliness. "No, I don't."

"Not a problem, I'll go grab one of mine. I just wanted to let you know I'm going to turn on the water out here."

"Okay. Let me know if you need anything," she replied.

A kiss would be nice, a little voice whispered in his head. Jeez, what in the hell was wrong with him? He didn't want a kiss from Eliza. All he wanted from her was a good, friendly neighbor kind of relationship and for her kids to forget about the "dead cat" in his backyard.

It took him nearly a half an hour to dig the hole deep enough. He placed the plant in the hole, shoveled soil all around it and then stood holding the hose over it so that it could get enough water to get a healthy start.

He was just about to finish up when the door opened and she stepped outside with a big glass of iced tea in her hand. "I thought you might need something cold to drink right about now."

"Thanks." He took the glass from her and swallowed a deep drink.

"It's so blazing hot out here," she said.

What was blazing hot was Eliza clad in a pair of cutoff jean shorts and a sleeveless pink blouse. "I'm used to the heat," he replied. "The peony should really do well here," he said in an effort to get his brain on the right path.

"All I know is it's really pretty right now and I thank you for it once again."

"Do your kids like pizza?"

"They love it." There was a touch of puzzlement in her eyes.

"I was wondering if I could take you and them out for some pizza on Friday night." Criminy, when had he been wondering that? What in the hell was happening to him? It was as if his mouth was working independent of his brain.

"Oh…that…that would be nice." The puzzlement in her eyes turned into pleasure.

He turned off the nozzle on the hose. "What time is good for you all?"

"Any time after four. That's when the kids get home from school."

"Then why don't we say about five?"

"Perfect." She gave him that smile that made him feel like he'd swallowed the sun.

"Okay, I'll just wrap up this hose and then I'll see you on Friday night."

Minutes later he walked across the lawn to his garage and put his shovel and the hose inside. He then went into the house and directly to the master bath. It was only when he was standing beneath a hot spray of water that he was able to fully process what had happened. He'd just made a date with the neighbor.

Chapter Three

A date. Was that what it was? Had Troy really asked her out on a date? Or was it merely a casual getting together of two neighbors? That was the question that played in Eliza's mind all day on Sunday and still plagued her as she sat at the kitchen table late-afternoon on Monday.

Mike the Mighty Mouseman had arrived minutes before and was now checking out the house for mice. She hoped he had a quick and easy way to get rid of the pesky critters that made far too much noise at night. His boots rang out on the hardwood floors overhead.

She glanced at the clock on the microwave. In just a few minutes she needed to leave to walk down the street to the bus stop. She'd already told Mike, and knowing he was a close friend of Troy's soothed any worries she might have about him being in the house all alone for a brief period of time.

Besides, the kids came home within minutes of each other and so she'd only be gone a short time. By the time she got back she hoped Mighty Mouse-man Mike would have a solid plan to rid the house of the little unwelcome occupants.

She waited until the very last minute and then got up and moved to the base of the stairs. "Mike, I'm leaving now," she called up.

He appeared at the top of the landing. "And I'm just about to make my way to your basement."

"I'll be right back," she said, and then headed for the front door.

It was as hot today as it had been all week. Summer in Kansas City could be quite unpleasant in August with high temperatures and humidity. She was definitely looking forward to fall, which was her favorite season and was usually glorious.

She couldn't help but think of Troy once again as she passed his house. It had to be tough to work outside on days like this, but she supposed he was used to the Midwestern weather.

When she reached the bus stop her heart lifted as it always did when she anticipated seeing her children after a day at school. Each afternoon they bubbled with excitement as they shared their tales of what had happened and what they had learned that day.

Today was no different. They chattered all the way back to the house. "There's a man here looking for mice," she said as they entered the front door. "His name is Mike, the Mighty Mouseman."

Apparently Mike was still in the basement. She and the kids headed to the kitchen for the usual after-school snack. Some days it was carrots and celery sticks, or apple slices and cheese. Today was the traditional cookies and milk.

The two had just settled in at the table with their treats before them when Mike appeared in the doorway. "Well, what have we here?" He smiled at the children. "Looks like a couple of cute little mice to me."

"We're not mice, we're kids," Katie said with a giggle. "Would you like a cookie, Mr. Mouse?" she asked with a sweet smile.

"Oh, no thank you, honey. I'm trying to watch my girlish figure." He laughed and patted the generous paunch around his middle.

"But you aren't a girl," Katie replied.

"Oh, it's just a saying," he replied.

"Like saying we look like cute mice is just a saying," Katie replied.

"Let's go into the living room and you can tell me what you've found," Eliza said, cutting off any further conversation between Mike and the kids. If Katie got stirred up she'd talk him into next week.

She led him into the living room where her sofa and end tables looked pitifully lost in the large space. The room begged for big overstuffed sofas and love seats, for wing-backed chairs and ornate mirrors and other accents.

And that wasn't all that the old house needed. Floors needed to be refinished and walls painted. The kitchen could use an updating, and dozens of other things needed some tender loving care. She'd managed to get the kids' rooms painted right after moving in, but the rest would have to be done a little at a time. Right now she was focused on mice.

"So, how bad is it?" she asked worriedly.

"It's not. In fact, I couldn't find any evidence that you have mice. There were no food trails, no droppings...nothing."

She stared at him for a long moment in surprise. "I thought for sure you were going to tell me we were being overrun by mice or some other kind of critters. Then what are all the noises we hear at night?"

"Troy told me you only moved into this house about a month ago. Is it possible you just aren't accustomed to the belches and groans an old, big house like this might make?"

"Maybe," she replied. "So, what do I owe you?"

"Nothing," he replied.

"Oh, surely I owe you something for your time and trouble," she protested.

He grinned at her. "I had time and this was no trouble. What do you think of my buddy Troy?"

Oh Lord, the warmth of a blush immediately swept over her cheeks. "He seems very nice, but I really don't know him that well. We've only had dinner together once."

One of Mike's bushy brown eyebrows quirked upward. "He had dinner with you?"

"Yes, and we're going out for pizza on Friday night."

He gazed at her for a long moment that became slightly uncomfortable and then he nodded and smiled. "That's a good thing. It's about time my man Troy climbed out of his self-imposed hell. He's a good guy who went through some really bad things. I hope this means he's finally found some forgiveness for himself." He glanced at his watch. "And now I need to get out of here. I've got an appointment in fifteen minutes across town."

Before she could fully process what she'd just learned about Troy, Mike was out the door.

"Did Mr. Mouse leave?"

Katie's voice whirled Eliza around. The little girl stood in the doorway, a smudge of chocolate just above her mouth. Her brother stood next to her with a milk mustache. "We're done with our cookies," Katie said. "Can we watch cartoons?"

"Both of you wash your face and hands and then you've got thirty minutes of television time before we get to homework."

As the kids disappeared to wash up, Eliza turned on the television and put in a DVD that had been borrowed from Sammy's school. It was a series of cartoons that was not only fun for Katie to watch, but also had narration that would help Sammy enjoy it as well.

Once the kids were settled on the sofa, she returned to the kitchen. As she cleaned up the snack dishes her mind whirred with questions about Troy. A self-imposed hell? What did that mean? And what kind of bad things had happened to him?

She was surprised to realize her interest was far more than the passing curiosity about a neighbor. Rather it was the interest of a woman in a man...a man she found wildly attractive. But just because she found him attractive and Mike's words about Troy had interested her didn't mean there would be any relationship with him. She definitely wasn't looking for a relationship.

The rest of the evening passed uneventfully and

soon it was time for bed. She tucked in Katie and then went to Sammy's room to do the same.

"Sleep tight," she said, and dropped a kiss on his cheek.

"Mommy, I've got something to tell you. I didn't want to say anything in front of Katie."

Eliza's heart jumped a beat. "What is it, honey? You know you can talk to me about anything."

"Last night Daddy was in my room."

Eliza stared at her son in surprise. "Honey, why would you think anyone was in your room last night?"

"I woke up because I heard some noise and I could tell by my Spidey senses that somebody was there, and he smelled just like Daddy."

"Sammy, you know that isn't possible. Your father passed away." She stroked a strand of hair away from his forehead, unable to believe they were having this conversation.

"Maybe it was Daddy's ghost," Sammy replied. "Do ghosts smell?"

"I suppose they might," she replied. There were times when Eliza thought she caught a faint scent of lilac that instantly evoked thoughts of her mother. She'd lost both of her parents in a car accident when she was twenty-one. In those brief moments of the lilac scent, she always imagined the spirit of her mother surrounding her with love.

"Were you scared?"

Sammy shook his head. "No, I didn't feel scared about it. If it was Daddy's ghost I figured maybe he just came to see how we were doing."

"But you know that if anything ever scares you in the night you can come wake me."

He smiled. "Duh, Mom. I know that."

"Now, enough talk about ghosts for one night. You need to get your sleep." She kissed him once again and then left his bedroom.

It wasn't until she was in bed and staring up at the dark ceiling that she finally had time to process everything the day had brought.

So, the house didn't have mice, but apparently it had a ghost who smelled like Blake. Eliza wasn't surprised that Sammy remembered what his father had smelled like. Blake had loved his cologne, a distinctive fragrance of cedar and patchouli, and he had always worn it liberally.

It was tragic that what Sammy couldn't remember was the gentle touch of his father's hand or the warmth of a father's kiss against his cheek.

Blake had seen Sammy as a hindrance, a child who required money and special attention that Blake, in his selfishness, wasn't willing to give.

If Blake hadn't left her when he had, she would have left him. The affairs he'd had were bad enough, but his inability to love his children had been the real deal-breaker.

Her thoughts shifted from one man to another. Troy. Mike's words about him whirled around in her head. What did he have to forgive himself for? Why had he been in a self-imposed hell? What had happened to him?

She had to be very careful who she invited into her life. She had her children to think about. She couldn't get romantically involved with anyone who might be here today and then gone tomorrow. She didn't want her children involved with anyone who might be a danger to them either physically or mentally.

She instantly chided herself. There was no reason to believe there was, or would be, anything romantic between herself and Troy. There was nothing wrong with neighbors just getting together for pizza.

A bump sounded, followed by a faint rustling, seeming to come from behind the far wall. She shot up to a sitting position, her heart beating frantically.

Quickly she reached out and turned on her bedside lamp.

She held her breath and waited. Silence. No other noises and nothing appeared amiss. She remained looking around and listening for several long minutes. She finally turned off the light and lay back down, her heart still banging an unsteady rhythm.

She hoped it was what Mike had suggested, that she just needed to get accustomed to the natural noises the old house made. But those noises didn't sound natural. They hadn't been the faint *whoosh* of the air conditioner or the sound of vents expanding. They had to be natural to the house because nothing else made sense. Still, it was a very long time before she finally drifted off back to sleep.

TROY STARED AT himself in the bathroom mirror. What in the hell did he think he was doing? In fifteen minutes he'd drive over to pick up Eliza and her kids for a pizza night.

He'd spoken to her yesterday when he'd caught her carrying in groceries. He'd asked her if they were still on for tonight and he'd almost hoped she'd cancel the plans.

But she hadn't. Instead her beautiful eyes had sparkled with a happy light as she told him she and the children were really looking forward to tonight.

He was looking forward to the night, too, and that disturbed him. He knew there would probably be laughter and he'd probably lust after Eliza, and he had no right to be happy or sexually attracted to anyone.

It had been years since he'd gotten ready for a date, but as he combed his hair and checked his jaw for any errant whiskers, a burn of excitement lit inside him.

He splashed on some cologne and then left the bathroom. *It's no big deal. A couple of hours*, he told himself. It was just pizza at a neighborhood pub. Soon he'd be back home and he could forget all about the neighbor lady with her children next door.

Thankfully, the kids had shown no further interest in the dead cat. He now had a nice heavy concrete birdbath in the spot. In the spring he'd plant flowers around it and hopefully nobody would ever dig up what was buried there.

It was precisely five o'clock when he rang Eliza's doorbell. Immediately she answered and the sight of her almost took his breath away.

Her jeans hugged the length of her long legs and the royal blue blouse she wore added a touch of that color to her lovely eyes. But it was the warmth and the beauty of her smile that punched him in the gut.

He felt himself respond with a wide smile of his own. "Ready for some pizza?"

"I'm ready, and I think the kids have been ready since yesterday morning when I told them about tonight," she replied. "Come on in. I'll just grab my purse from the kitchen."

He followed behind her into the large foyer and within minutes they were all together, the kids dancing around the two adults with excitement.

"What kind of pizza do you like, Mr. Anderson?" Katie asked once they were in his car.

"My favorite is pepperoni," he replied. "And you can call me Troy."

"Mom, that's your favorite, too. Isn't that nice that you both like the same thing, Mr. Troy?" Katie said. "You two make a good couple."

He cast a glance over at Eliza and smiled at her. It was obvious Katie was attempting her hand at a little matchmaking. Eliza gave him a helpless, slightly embarrassed smile of her own.

It didn't matter how much matchmaking Katie attempted, a match wasn't going to happen between the two of them. This was just a pleasant neighborly outing and that was all. No matter how interesting he found Eliza and no matter how much he lusted after her, tonight was the beginning and the ending of any sort of relationship except a friendly nod in passing.

"What kind of pizza do you like, Sammy?" he asked.

"Just plain cheese," he replied.

"That's what I like, too," Katie added. "We all

love pizza. Sometimes Mommy makes us homemade pizza, but it's always fun to go out for it."

Minutes later he pulled into the parking lot of Garozzi's Pizza. The small establishment was in a strip mall and served not only pizza but also Italian favorites like lasagna and other pasta dishes. It was a rather small, intimate place with candles on the tables and booths and soft, unobtrusive music playing overhead.

It didn't take long for them to settle in a booth and for the waitress, Tabitha, to greet them. "Hey, Troy. Is this your family?"

"No," Eliza replied quickly. "We're just neighbors."

"But they're the perfect couple 'cause they both love pepperoni pizza," Katie quipped.

Tabitha laughed. "And that's what's important in a relationship, right, kiddo?" She took their orders and then left their booth.

"This obviously isn't your first time in here," Eliza said minutes later when they were waiting for their pizza and they'd been served their drinks.

"Actually, I come in here pretty often. It's easier to stop in here for dinner than going home and cooking after working all day," he replied. "The prices are good, the food is excellent and I don't have to eat my own cooking."

"So, am I to take away from that information that you aren't much of a cook?" she asked.

He grinned. "I can cook just enough to keep myself alive."

"Mom is an awesome cook," Sammy said.

"I figured that out after just eating with you all one time," Troy replied.

"Oh, it's easy to be a good cook with a Crock-Pot," she protested. "But I have to admit I am a decent cook."

Before long the pizza arrived and Troy found himself wishing he'd had this meal with just Eliza. It was difficult to really talk to her with the two children present.

However, he did enjoy the laughter Sammy and Katie added to the meal. He learned Katie wanted to be an actress when she grew up and her favorite foods included mac and cheese and ice cream with pink sprinkles.

Sammy's favorite foods were cheeseburgers, pizza and chocolate chip cookies that his mother baked. He didn't know what he wanted to be when he grew up, but he liked puzzle questions and math.

What Troy didn't learn was what had happened to Eliza's marriage, or how difficult it must be to raise a blind son. He would have liked to find out what her favorite color was and what else might make her happy besides her children.

Then he inwardly shook himself for wanting to know all those things about her. He needed to stay in his own lane where she was concerned.

Still, it was a fun night that ended too quickly as far as he was concerned. As they stepped out of the pizza place to head to his car in the parking lot, a little hand slipped into his.

He froze, thrown back to the last time he'd felt a small hand in his. He gazed down at the little girl next to him and for a brief moment he had a flash of dancing blond curls and bright blue eyes.

An exuberant happiness filled him, dashed quickly by a stab of pain as the vision of his daughter quickly faded away. "Mr. Troy, thank you for the pizza," Katie said, and then released her hold on his fingers.

"Yes, thank you," Sammy echoed. He walked right next to his mother, his hand on her arm as he navigated the unfamiliar ground to get to the car.

"You're welcome, and it's nice that you both have such good manners," he said.

"Mommy believes good manners are very important," Sammy said.

"I agree with her." He shot Eliza a smile. God, she was so pretty and didn't even seem aware of her own attractiveness. The night had seemed so easy, so effortless with her.

They got back into the car, and before long he pulled up in her driveway. The kids ran ahead of them to the front door. "Thank you, Troy," she said as she pulled her keys out of her purse. "Both of you get your jammies on. You can have a half an hour of television time before bed," she said as she unlocked the door. Sammy and Katie ran inside and she turned back to face him.

"It was a fun evening."

"It was. Your children are great kids and both of them seem very bright."

She laughed. "Thank you. I think so, but I'm more than a little biased where they are concerned."

"As you should be." When she laughed like that, when she smiled, he wanted to get closer to her. Something about her definitely drew him to her.

Dusk had begun to fall, painting her features in a warm golden light. Would it be bad manners to steal a kiss without asking permission first? He so wanted to kiss her. Without thinking any more about it he simply leaned forward and captured her mouth with his.

Her lips were warm and inviting. Even though he wanted to wrap her in his arms and pull her closer to him, despite the fact that he wanted to deepen the kiss, he kept it light and fast.

"Thanks, Eliza, for a great evening," he said when he broke the kiss and stepped back from her.

Her features radiated surprise and her cheeks took on the pink hue of a blush, but she didn't look displeased by his kiss. "Good night, Troy." She slipped into the house and closed the door behind her.

He returned to his car and pulled into his own driveway. His heart was light. He felt…happy. He hadn't felt like this in years. He unlocked his front door and went directly to his recliner chair and sat.

He replayed the evening in his mind, smiling as he thought of the laughter they had all shared. He hadn't been kidding when he'd told her both the kids were bright, and they also both had a great sense of humor.

The night had only whetted his appetite to learn more about Eliza, to spend more time with her. And he thought she might feel the same way about him.

It was as if he suffered from some sort of split personality disorder where she was concerned. Part of him wanted to explore the crazy-good feelings she gave him, but the other part warned him away.

Thoughts of that moment when Katie had slipped her hand into his intruded. Instantly a vision of another little girl filled his head.

Annie.

A special kind of agony filled him. What in the hell was he doing feeling happy…looking for more happiness when he didn't deserve it? The last thing Eliza and her children needed in their lives was him.

He was a monster and wasn't good for anyone. There were days he wasn't sure he could live with himself.

He didn't deserve anything good because the bottom line was that he'd killed his daughter.

Chapter Four

"I like Mr. Troy," Katie said as Eliza tucked her in later that evening.

"He seems like a very nice man," Eliza agreed. And the nice man's kiss had both surprised and electrified her. She'd scarcely had time to process it since she'd been home.

"Good night, sweetheart," she said to her daughter and planted a kiss on her forehead. "Sleep tight."

"Night, Mommy," Katie replied.

She'd already tucked in Sammy so she headed directly into her own bedroom. It wasn't until she was in bed that she permitted herself to think again about the delicious, heart-stopping and all-too-brief kiss.

Why had he done it? It had definitely changed the relationship from friendly neighbors to something more. But what was he looking for from her? And why was she so excited to find out?

She reached up and touched her lips, remembering the wonderful sensation of his mouth over hers. His lips had been soft and tender, yet with a sense of command that had been thrilling. A shiver raced through her as she wondered what it would be like to share a longer, deeper kiss with Troy.

He hadn't mentioned going out again. He hadn't even mentioned seeing her again. Maybe the kiss hadn't meant anything to him. Perhaps it had just been a friendly peck as far as he was concerned. She shouldn't get ahead of herself thinking about doing it again with him.

Still, the kiss had reminded her that she was more than a mom. She was more than just a good website designer. She was a woman who had been alone for a long time. Troy had awakened the woman inside her.

And it was definitely thrilling to remember that woman.

It was equally thrilling to think about what might come next with Troy. But she was smart enough to realize there might be nothing more to come with him.

And should she even be thinking about opening herself up once again to a man? Blake had hurt her so badly, and her instinct was to guard her heart.

And it wasn't just about her anymore, it was also about her children. Right now they were happy kids.

Did she really want to bring in somebody else who might mess things up?

She turned over on her side and drifted off to sleep. She awakened suddenly, her heart beating frantically and all her nerves on high alert.

She sat up, still a bit groggy, but something had pulled her from her dreams. What was it? An unusually loud house noise? Her eyes adjusted to the dark and she saw nothing amiss. A glance at the clock on the nightstand let her know it was just after two.

Maybe it had just been a nightmare that had suddenly awakened her. That had to be it. She was about to relax back into her pillow when a big dark silhouette moved past her bedroom doorway.

Her stomach clenched and the taste of terror rose up in the back of her mouth. Somebody was in her house. Oh dear God, she needed to get to her children.

On shaky legs, she slid out of the bed and stood. She kept her scream of fear locked deep in the back of her throat. The last thing she wanted was to scare her children or to have a confrontation with whoever had invaded her home in the dead of night. She needed to be as quiet as possible.

What did the person want? Why was he in her house? She was relatively sure it was a male by the height and general size of the silhouette.

Any other thoughts she might have considered vanished beneath the agonizing need for her to make sure Sammy and Katie were safe. She crept to her doorway and peered out. To her right was the stairs, one set going up to the third floor and the other going down to the main level.

Where had he gone? Even though she saw nobody at the moment, her heart still crashed painfully hard against her ribs. She needed to get her children to safety, and this place was no longer safe.

She went directly across the hall to Sammy's room. She hurried to his bedside and gave his shoulder a little shake. "Sammy, honey…wake up and be very quiet."

He sat up. "Is it morning?" he whispered.

"No, it's the middle of the night. We're going to be as quiet as we can and we're going next door to Mr. Troy's house." She didn't know when she'd made the plan to get out of her home and into Troy's, but she hoped they'd all be safe there. Or would they? Maybe it was Troy who had broken in. She immediately dismissed the idea. The silhouette she'd seen had been too tall, too bulky to be Troy's. She had to believe they'd all be safe at his house. She just wanted to get out of here.

Thank goodness Sammy didn't ask any questions. He immediately got out of bed and together they went into Katie's room. She roused her daughter from sleep and together the three of them crept down the stairs.

With each step they took her legs shook and every nerve in her body screamed. What would she do if they met whoever was in the house? She had no weapon, but she'd fight him tooth and nail to assure the safety of her children.

Thankfully they encountered nobody, but that didn't slow Eliza's heartbeat or stanch the bitter taste of fear that rose up from the back of her throat.

She had no idea where the man might be. She didn't even know for sure that he was still in the house, but she wasn't taking any chances. She'd been so frantic to get to her children she hadn't even taken time to grab her cell phone on the nightstand next to her bed.

She unlocked her front door and they all stepped outside. The night was hot, but cold chills raced up and down her spine as they left the house and hurried across the lawn to Troy's place. With a glance back at her house, she knocked on Troy's door.

It took several hard knocks before he opened the door. His sleepy eyes widened in surprise. "Eliza…"

"Can we come in?" Desperation made her voice higher in tone than normal.

Without a question, he opened the door and ushered them inside. The minute he locked the door behind them she breathed a shuddery sigh of utter relief. "Can you call the police? Somebody is in my house," she said in a low tone. The last thing she wanted was to frighten Sammy and Katie.

"Done," he replied. He looked at the children and then back at her. "Make yourself at home and I'll go make the call."

He disappeared into what she assumed was the kitchen as she directed her children to the oversize brown leather sofa. Within seconds the two were curled into the corners of the sofa and were sound asleep.

A fierce tremor worked through her, a tremor of relief. And with their assured safety came other thoughts. She should have grabbed a robe. All she had on was a midnight-blue silk nightgown that showed far more skin than she wanted her neighbor or the police to see. At least he'd had on a robe and a pair of long black-and-white-plaid sleep pants.

Jeez, why was she worrying about clothing when there was a man in her house in the middle of the night? What was wrong with her? Had she lost her mind?

What had the man wanted? Why was he there? Had he been there to rob her? Ha, the joke was on him. Other than her computer equipment there was nothing of any real value in the entire house. She'd even sold her wedding ring to a pawnshop when her marriage ended.

Troy walked back into the living room. "The police should be here in just a few minutes." His voice was low and soft. "Here, take this." He shrugged out of his robe and handed it to her.

"Thank you," she said gratefully. She stood and quickly wrapped herself in the navy terry-cloth robe that smelled vaguely like his attractive cologne and a hint of fabric softener.

"I'm sorry about bothering you in the middle of the night, but I was terrified and just wanted to get my children to safety." She sat back down between the two sleeping kids.

"So, what happened?" He eased down in the recliner chair across from her.

"I was sleeping and something awakened me. I thought it might have been some sort of a house noise. I sat up and waited to see if I'd hear it again…" The back of her throat began to squeeze tight and a new chill swept through her. "And then a man walked past my bedroom doorway."

Troy leaned forward, his features radiating a hint of alarm. "Did you recognize the man?"

"No, it was too dark. All I saw was a silhouette. Whoever it was, he was tall and a little bit thick in the body. And all I could think about was Sammy and Katie and getting them out of there." Before she could say anything more, there was a knock on the door.

"That will be the police," Troy said, and got up to answer. "It must be a slow night for them and they must have been in the area to get here so quickly."

She jumped up off the sofa and hurried after him. Two police officers stood in the large foyer. She quickly told them about the man in her house and that the front door of her home was unlocked.

They left immediately with the promise that they'd be back after they'd checked things out. "Why don't we move the kids into one of my guest rooms?" Troy suggested when the officers had left. "You all might as well stay here for the rest of the night."

"Oh, I can't impose any more than I already have on you," she protested. But the idea of not having to go back inside her house in the dark was definitely appealing.

"Nonsense, it's no trouble at all. Can they sleep together in the same bed?"

"Actually I would prefer it that way." Sammy would be disoriented when he woke up in a strange bed in an unknown place, but he could always depend on his older sister to navigate the way for him.

If the circumstances were different she'd put

Sammy in bed with her, so she could be there for him in the morning when he woke up in a strange place. However, there was no way she intended to go to bed now. At the moment she felt as if she might never, ever sleep again.

They walked back into the living room. "If you don't mind getting Sammy, I can carry Katie," she said, giving in to his generous offer.

He picked up the sleeping boy in his arms while she got Katie. "What are we doing, Mommy?" Katie asked sleepily.

"We're spending the night with Mr. Troy."

"Oh, that's fun. Did you tell him we like him?" she asked.

"Yes, honey," Eliza replied. "I told him."

"That's good." Katie closed her eyes and fell back asleep.

Eliza followed Troy up the stairs to an attractive bedroom decorated in shades of blue. With Sammy still in his arms, he managed to pull down the spread and place the sleeping boy on light blue sheets. Eliza did the same with Katie and breathed a sigh of relief that she wasn't going to have to rouse the children from their sleep again for the rest of the night.

"You can use this room," he said, and stepped across the hall and turned on the light to reveal another guest room, this one decorated in cheerful shades of yellow.

"Thank you, this is very nice of you," she replied.

It wasn't until she was following Troy back down the stairs that she processed the fact that when he'd given her his robe, it had left him bare-chested. She'd been so into her own head she hadn't noticed it until now.

Just what she needed…to be caught in the middle of the night with a half-naked man who had unexpectedly kissed her only hours before while she waited for the police to tell her if somebody was still in her house. It was all so surreal.

He returned to the recliner while she sat on the edge of the sofa to wait for the police officers to return from her house.

"Would you like something to drink?" he asked. "I imagine you could use a good stiff one right about now."

"That does sound good, but the last thing I want is for alcohol to be on my breath when the police come back."

A knock sounded at the door. "Speaking of…" Troy jumped up to answer.

Seconds later he returned with the two officers behind him. Eliza stood. "Did you find anyone?"

"We did a thorough search of the house and didn't

find anyone inside," the officer with the name badge identifying him as Doug Wilkins said.

"We need to get some information from you," Officer Gary Dickenson added. He motioned her to sit and then pulled a pad and pen from his pocket.

He asked her some general questions and then asked her exactly what had happened. She explained about something awakening her and then seeing the silhouette pass by her bedroom door.

"So you were asleep right before you saw this figure," Officer Wilkins said.

"No, I was wide-awake," she countered.

"But is it possible you were still groggy and the figure might have been part of a dream?" he asked.

"No, that isn't what happened. I was wide-awake when I saw him." Tension began to coil in her stomach. Didn't they believe her?

"We need to have you return to the house with us to see if anything has been stolen," Officer Dickenson said.

She looked at Troy. "Go ahead," he said, and offered her an assuring smile. "I'll stay here with the kids."

"Do you have any idea who might have come into your house? An ex-husband or boyfriend?" Officer Wilkins asked as they stepped out Troy's front door. "Is there anyone who might have a key?"

"No, my ex-husband is dead and there is no boy-friend." She pulled Troy's robe more tightly around her despite the warmth of the night. "Nobody has a key to the house except me."

Her house rose up in front of her, suddenly alien and spooky-looking in the moonlight. Would she ever feel safe there again?

"There is somebody who has had a problem with me," she said suddenly when they reached her front porch. "His name is Leon Whitaker. I backed out of making a web page for him and he's been harassing me by text and email ever since."

"What do you mean by harassing?" Officer Wilkins asked.

"He tells me he's going to ruin my business and destroy my life…things like that. I just thought he was a nuisance, but maybe he's more dangerous than I thought."

"Does he know where you live?" Officer Dick-enson opened the front door and ushered her inside.

"I don't think so. I met him at a coffee shop when we initially talked about the project." A new shiver worked up her spine. Was it possible that he had fol-lowed her home from that meeting? Did he know where she lived and now intended to terrorize her in person rather than by email and text? How dan-gerous was the man?

"Let's look around and see if anything has been stolen and then we'll take down any information you have about this Whitaker fellow," Officer Dickenson said.

It didn't take long for her to confirm to the officers that nothing had been stolen. She didn't have much information to give them about Leon, only his name and phone number. She didn't know his home address.

She grabbed her purse from the kitchen table and then locked the front door behind all of them as they left to return to Troy's.

"And you're sure the front door was locked when you and the children went to leave the house?" Officer Wilkins asked.

"Positive, why?" Once again, tension wound tight in her stomach.

"We could find no point of entry for somebody to get inside. All your doors and windows were locked up tight and showed no evidence of any tampering, and there appears to be no sign of an intruder being inside," Officer Dickenson said. "Are you positively sure you weren't asleep?"

They didn't believe her. "I was awake," she replied firmly. She could swear she was awake when she'd seen the figure go past her doorway.

They reached Troy's porch and she turned back

to look at the two officers. "I'm sorry that I bothered you. Thank you for your prompt response."

"Don't apologize. This is our job," Officer Wilkins replied. "Don't hesitate to call if anything else comes up," he added.

She returned to the living room to find Troy seated in the recliner. He stood at the sight of her. "Everything all right?"

"Not really," she said honestly. She sat on the sofa and he sank back down in the recliner. "There was no point of entry found and nothing had been stolen."

"Thank goodness for that," he replied.

"They didn't believe me, Troy. They think I'm just a foolish, hysterical woman who dreamed I saw somebody and overreacted."

She shook her head and released a deep sigh of frustration. "All the doors and windows were locked. I don't know, maybe I really was still asleep. Maybe it was just a strange cast of the moon or the remnants of a dream that made me believe I saw a figure pass my bedroom doorway."

She'd been so sure of what she'd seen until the police had told her there was no sign of any point of entry. Had she been asleep? If she hadn't been, then a man had somehow gotten into her house in the dark of night. How had he gotten in? What had he been doing there?

And more importantly, what had he wanted and would he be back?

Troy didn't know Eliza very well, but even a stranger would be able to see the stress that tightened her delicate features and the residue of fear that darkened her eyes. "Pick your poison," he said, and stood. "I've got scotch and whiskey and both red and white wine."

"Normally I'd say a glass of white wine, but I think tonight calls for a little something stronger. A scotch on the rocks?"

"Ah, a woman after my own heart. I'll be right back." He left the living room and entered his kitchen. His liquor was kept in a cabinet next to the sink and he bent down and grabbed the bottle of scotch.

There had been a time two and a half years ago when scotch had become too much of a familiar friend to him. He'd tried to drown his bad memories and pain in nights of boozing. But when he realized there was no peace, no forgiveness in the bottom of a bottle, he'd stopped the bad habit. He only drank occasionally now.

As he worked to make the drinks, he tried to ignore the slow burn in the pit of his belly. It was a burn ignited by the vision of Eliza with her gorgeous hair loose around her shoulders and wearing his robe. She'd looked sexy in her nightgown, but something about his robe around her was even sexier. He'd never been jealous of a robe before.

With the drinks in hand, he returned to the living room. He handed one to her and carried the second one back to the recliner.

"I need to apologize once again for disrupting your night," she said.

She appeared so charmingly earnest. "Please stop," he replied. "Besides, this is what good neighbors do for each other."

It had to be well after three in the morning, but he was wide-awake and she didn't look a bit sleepy either. He took a drink and then asked, "Tell me about your marriage…about what happened to it."

Jeez, what was he doing? Why did he want to know everything he could learn about her? Why did he want to know about her past and about what made her laugh and what made her cry? She wasn't a woman to be toyed with, especially since she had two small children.

These things shot through his head in the blink of an eye, and then were overridden by a saner voice reminding him that he'd just asked her a simple question. He hadn't suggested they jump into his bed together.

Besides, talking about that might help take her mind off the scare she'd just had. He was actually doing her a favor.

She took a drink and then released a deep sigh. "I met Blake at a friend's birthday party. He was attractive and funny and he spent the next six weeks sweeping me off my feet and within three months we were married." A frown danced between her neatly shaped eyebrows. "I probably wouldn't have married him so quickly if I hadn't been grieving over my parents' deaths. They were killed in a car accident two months before I met Blake."

She took another drink and then continued. "Anyway, fast forward a year and we had Katie. My only real complaint at that time was that Blake wasn't a good and present parent. He still liked to party and I thought it was time for him to grow up. We fought a lot about it and finally I told Blake I was ready to walk out of the marriage and he promised to be a better husband and father. I got pregnant again and when we learned the baby was a boy, Blake seemed delighted. But when Sammy was born blind, Blake was bitterly disappointed and wanted nothing to do with his son. I think that was when he started cheating on me. Anyway, Sammy was a little over two when I was ready to leave the marriage, but Blake beat me to it and served me divorce papers. He immediately left to stay with friends in Florida and then a year after he moved I learned he'd died in a motorcycle wreck."

She slapped her hand over her mouth. "Oh my goodness, I'm so sorry that I've just been rambling on."

"Don't apologize, and I'm sorry about your husband's death," Troy said. He wondered if she was aware of how her facial features spoke her emotions. She'd told the story very matter-of-factly, but her expressions as she'd told him of the cheating and her husband's lack of love toward the children had been of deep pain and anger.

"Thanks. I never wished him dead, but I certainly wished him out of my life for Katie's and Sammy's sakes. His continued rejection of them would have eventually harmed them irreparably." Her eyes blazed for a moment. "I won't let anything or anyone hurt my kids."

For a moment Troy couldn't find his voice as he thought of his own daughter and how careless he'd been with her life. Eliza would have never, ever been so careless.

"I'm sorry to admit it, but any love I felt for Blake turned into hate by the time we separated. Of course, the kids will never know my real feelings for their father." She gave a small laugh and shook her head. "I'm sorry. Not only have I been rambling on, but I'm also keeping you from sleep."

"I'm still not a bit sleepy, but if you're ready to call it a night, please feel free to go on upstairs."

"I'm still wound up too tight to go to sleep," she replied. "I just can't imagine who might have been in my house and why they were there."

"What do you know about the old man who lived there?" he asked, grateful that the conversation had moved on from children before he began to fall into dark thoughts of his past.

"Frank?" She shrugged her slender shoulders. "Not much. I know he raised Blake and I met him a few times. Even though he raised Blake the two didn't seem to be very close."

"I heard a few rumors from some of the other neighbors that Frank Malone was once some kind of a mobster."

"Really?" She sat up straighter. "Blake certainly never told me that about his grandfather."

Troy shrugged. "I'm not even sure if it's true. It was just a rumor I heard when I first bought my house."

"Still, that might explain the secret stairway and the hiding places the kids have found in the house.

Maybe I need to do a little research into the late Frank Malone."

"What about Blake's parents?" he asked curiously. "If Blake was raised by his grandfather then what happened to his parents?"

"According to Blake, his mother, Frank's daughter, and his father got into drugs real bad. They were homeless a lot and eventually they dropped Blake off at Frank's when he was five years old and he never heard from or saw them again."

"That's tough," Troy replied. "So you don't know if they're dead or alive."

"I don't have a clue." She frowned. "Maybe I need to check them out, too. If they're alive and got sober they might be real upset that I inherited the house, but you'd think they would have protested the will or whatever by now." She relaxed back into the sofa and eyed him curiously. "I've told you all about my failed marriage. Now it's your turn. Why did your marriage end?"

He stared at her as an old despair lodged inside his chest, tightening to the point he wasn't sure he would be able to speak. He swallowed hard and then began his tale. "My marriage ended when my daughter was kidnapped and killed and it was all my fault."

He hadn't expected to say those words; rather, they had exploded out of him as if from under an enormous pressure. He continued to stare at her, both appalled and yet oddly relieved. It was the first time he'd uttered those words aloud to anyone in the three years since Annie's murder.

"Oh, Troy," she said softly.

He looked down into his glass. "It was a normal Saturday morning and it was our routine for Daddy and Annie to go to the arcade while Mommy got her hair and nails done." It had always been precious father-daughter time, just the two of them hanging out while Mommy was busy.

At that time Troy had worked long hours growing his business, but he was always available on Saturdays to spend time with his daughter and she was always so excited about the day of Daddy time. He looked forward to those times, too. Children grew up so fast and he was determined to enjoy as much time as possible with his daughter.

He paused and downed the last of the liquid in his glass, wishing he could drink enough that he would forever forget that in the blink of an eye he'd lost his sweet Annie forever. But he'd been there and tried that and it hadn't worked. Nothing worked as an escape from this agony.

He placed the glass on a nearby end table and then stood, unable to sit still as he told her the whole ugly story. And when he was finished, she would probably look at him with disgust and not want anything more to do with him. And maybe that would be the best for both of them.

He stared at the wall to the left of where she sat on the sofa. "We went to the neighborhood arcade as usual. Annie loved the arcade. Anyway, we'd been there about an hour when I noticed they'd put in a new pinball machine. I normally didn't play the machines, but instead always watched Annie play, but I decided to play that damned pinball machine."

For a moment his head filled with the flashing lights and *boink*s and *ping*s of the machine. "Play it, Daddy," Annie had said. And he had. He'd been completely caught up in the game.

He attempted to draw in a deep breath, but it caught painfully in his chest. He began to pace as all the memories of that horrible day pierced through him.

Annie had worn a pink blouse with a purple pair of shorts…her two favorite colors. A ribbon held her thick blond hair in a ponytail that bobbed and bounced with her every movement. She had been such a pretty child with her mother's blond coloring and Troy's mouth and bright blue eyes.

"I only took my eyes off her for a minute or two, but that's all it took. I finished the game and when I turned around she was gone." He stopped pacing as the hollow wind of despair rushed through him. "They found her body the next day in a trash bin two blocks away from the arcade."

When he'd first been unable to find her, he'd screamed her name over and over again in the arcade, frantic to find her. It didn't take him long to realize she was nowhere in the building.

The police had arrived and asked to see the surveillance tapes only to discover the equipment had malfunctioned a week before and hadn't been fixed.

Troy had gone outside, still screaming her name as he searched for any sign of his little girl. He'd called Sherry, who had joined the frantic search. That had been the longest, most horrifying night of his life.

To his horror, tears now pressed hot at his eyes, and the back of his throat closed up. All of his stomach muscles clenched tight and he knew he couldn't hold back the raw emotions that ripped through him.

"Oh, Troy." Eliza jumped up off the sofa and reached for him. She pulled him into her arms and he held her tight as his tears began to fall.

He'd thought he'd cried all he could when Annie had first gone missing. He'd believed he'd sobbed out the last of his tears when her little body had been found tossed away in a trash bin and later when they'd laid her to rest.

These tears were different from the ones he'd

cried at those times. His crying now was less intense and prompted by a deep, profound sadness that he knew would always be with him.

It didn't take long before he managed to pull himself together. He released his hold on Eliza and stepped back from her. "God, I'm so sorry," he said with a mixture of both embarrassment and humiliation. "I didn't know I was going to do that. I... I've never done that before in front of anyone."

"Please don't apologize." She reached out and grabbed his hand and guided him to the sofa where they both sat. He swiped a hand through his hair. He drew in a deep breath and then slowly released it. "Anyway, Sherry, my wife, couldn't abide to even look at me afterward. She blamed me and within three months she was gone, too."

"Did they ever catch the person responsible?" Eliza asked. She leaned toward him and her evocative scent filled his head, and for some inexplicable reason it brought him a modicum of comfort.

"They got him. His name is Dwight Weatherby. He's a known sex offender, a pedophile, and when the police questioned him they saw Annie's hair ribbons on his coffee table." His stomach clenched once again, this time with a hint of the rage that had prompted him to walk a line outside of the law.

"I hope he's now rotting in a prison somewhere."

"No, he isn't. He's walking around as free as a bird." He couldn't help the bitterness that crept into his voice.

Eliza gasped. "How is that possible?" She reached out and took his hand once again.

"A woman friend of his alibied him for the time of the kidnapping and insisted the hair ribbons were her daughter's. The prosecutor refused to take the case because there just wasn't enough evidence. But I know he's guilty. I saw a picture of those ribbons and they were in Annie's hair the day I took her to the arcade. I tied those ribbons in her hair myself and they weren't just plain pink, they had pale purple edges, and they were missing when she was found in that dumpster."

Eliza squeezed his hand. Her eyes were a deep smoky gray with a softness, a compassion he hadn't realized he'd hungered for until this very moment. "I should have never played that damned game. I should have never taken my eyes off her for a single second. I was careless with her. I got her killed."

"Troy, you can't blame yourself for this. It happened because of an evil man, not because of anything you did wrong. It wasn't your fault."

He fell into her soft gaze and all he could think about was his need to kiss her, to connect with her in a way that would vanquish his guilt and take the edge off his grief.

She seemed to sense his need, for she leaned forward and he captured her soft lips with his. The gentle kiss they shared wasn't enough. He touched the edge of her lower lip with his tongue, seeking entry.

She met his tongue with hers and just that quickly the flames of desire burned hot inside him. He leaned back and pulled her closer to his body as the kiss continued.

Her heart beat as quickly as his own, a rapid tattoo that encouraged him to slide his hands beneath his robe and to roam up and down her back against the cool silk of her nightgown.

All rational thought fell away as he gave himself to the moment, and the only woman who had offered him any kind of redemption, the redemption he hadn't received from anyone else, including himself.

Her scent surrounded him, torching his desire even hotter as his lips claimed hers once again. He wanted her with a hunger he couldn't ever remember feeling for any other woman.

She was so soft, so giving, and he wanted to lose himself in her. All he could think about was how much he'd like to take her right now.

"Eliza." He whispered her name softly as his

mouth left hers. He wanted to get lost in the undeniable, overwhelming desire he had for her.

"Troy, we can't. Not here and not now." Her words pierced through the veil of his arousal and he instantly raised his hands from her.

She sat up and the look she gave him was one of both regret and promise. "I'm sorry, Troy. It's been such a crazy night and I don't think..."

"It's all right. Don't apologize." He gave her a reassuring smile. She was right. It had been a crazy night and he didn't want to take her like a lusty teenager on the sofa. And when he did make love to her he wanted to be sure she was as into it as he would be. He wanted her head to be completely clear when they went to bed together.

It had been an emotional night for both of them and he didn't want those emotions to drive her to do something she really didn't want to do. When they made love he wanted no regrets.

Would he have reacted with such desire to any available woman? Would he have even told another woman about Annie and his guilt? Somehow he didn't think so. There was just something special about Eliza.

One thing was for certain: if somebody had been in her house...somebody who intended her or her children harm, come hell or high water, Troy intended to be there to protect them.

He would do for them what he hadn't done for his daughter and maybe...just maybe in protecting them he would finally find a bit of forgiveness for himself.

Chapter Five

The next morning Troy walked them home after a breakfast of fresh doughnuts he'd picked up from the local bakery before anyone else was awake.

The kids were delighted with the sugary meal, but were disappointed that they'd slept through the fun of a slumber party with the neighbor.

"We need to have another slumber party when Sammy and I are awake," Katie said as they walked across the lawn. "Maybe next time you could spend the night at our house, Mr. Troy. We could play games and have popcorn and ice cream."

Troy looked at Eliza and grinned. His blue eyes twinkled with a bit of mischief. "That sounds like fun, but it would be up to your mom."

She knew what he was thinking about and she'd scarcely stopped thinking about it since the moment she'd opened her eyes that morning...that unbridled desire that had nearly exploded out of control between them the night before.

"What about it, Mom? When can Mr. Troy come over and spend the night with us?" Sammy asked.

"We'll just have to wait and see," she replied, and kept her gaze off Troy. Everything between them suddenly felt as if it were happening too fast. Granted, they had learned a lot about each other the night before, but she'd really known him for only a week.

Besides, she didn't know how much of her own fear combined with his heartbreaking past had stoked the explosive desire inside her. Would she have fallen into his arms so easily if she hadn't been scared out of her house? Would she have kissed him with such passion if he hadn't shared the tragic events of his past? She really didn't know.

The one thing she did know was that she wasn't ready to fall into bed with anyone. There was no question there was a huge amount of lust between them, but she wasn't comfortable exploring that with him right now. It was just too soon.

"Why don't you show me around your house?" he suggested when she unlocked the front door. She smiled at him gratefully. She had a feeling he didn't care about seeing her home, but rather wanted to assure them both that nobody was inside.

"I can show you my room, Mr. Troy," Katie said eagerly. She grabbed hold of his hand and pulled him toward the stairs. "I've got a pink room with lots of dolls."

He laughed as they went up, with Eliza and Sammy following behind. He looked at Katie's room and oohed and aahed over the frilly pink bedspread and the dolls that were seated at the small pink-and-purple plastic table. He showed endless patience as Katie introduced each doll to him one by one.

"What a nice shade of blue," he said when they entered Sammy's room. He stopped and looked at Eliza, obviously appalled by his reference to a color Sammy couldn't see. "I'm sorry, Sammy."

Sammy smiled and sat on the edge of his bed. "Don't be sorry, Mr. Troy. I've got different colors in my head. Katie gave me different colors."

"I told him green looks like the way celery tastes. Blue looks the way blueberries taste," Katie explained.

"Yellow looks like the sun when it warms your face," Sammy continued. "I don't know if the colors in my imagination are right or not, but at least Katie and Mom help me see things differently. Mom says I have a great imagination."

"I'm sure you do," Troy replied.

"Come on, Sammy. Come into my room and play dolls with me," Katie said.

When the kids left Sammy's room, Troy checked Sammy's closet as he had done in Katie's room. He closed the door and then turned to look at Eliza.

"Your children are absolutely amazing."

She smiled. "They are, aren't they?"

"And now I'd like to check out your bedroom."

Her bed was a double, not a king, and she wondered if he noticed that the peach-colored dust ruffle was frayed and worn. "Looks cozy," he said.

The words appeared to have been said innocently enough, but the vision they evoked in her head was definitely X-rated. It was far too easy to imagine the two of them naked and cozy beneath the peach-colored sheets. She quickly shoved the image out of her head.

"Do you mind if I check in your closet?" he asked.

"Go for it. I'd appreciate it," she replied.

When they were finished in her room, they headed for the stairs. "What's up there?" he asked, and gestured upward.

"Three large bedrooms and a bathroom. I don't have anything in any of the rooms up there," she replied.

"Then it should just take me a minute or two to

check them out." He didn't wait for her response, but instead took the stairs two at a time.

Eliza leaned against the wall and released a deep sigh. How did she get so lucky to have a neighbor who was going above and beyond to make sure she and her children had nothing to fear? There was no question she would rest easier knowing Troy had checked out the house.

Aside from the obvious physical attraction she had for him, his kindness to her and her children definitely drew her to him. She would have liked to make a pot of coffee and invite him to linger for more conversation, but it was Saturday and she knew he probably had work to do. She'd already taken up enough of his time in landing on his doorstep in the middle of the night. She'd been enough of a burden to Troy in the past twenty-four hours. She didn't need to bother him anymore.

Besides, she also had a big project to work on and a timeline for completion that was approaching far too quickly. She definitely needed to get some work done today as well.

He came back down the stairs and gave her a reassuring smile. "Everything looks fine."

"Thank you for coming in and checking it all out," she replied as they walked toward the front door.

"No problem." When they reached the door he

turned back to her. His eyes twinkled as he reached out and lightly touched the tip of her nose. "Just let me know when you're ready for that slumber party. I'm available anytime."

She laughed and gave him a teasing tap on the shoulder and then sobered. "Thanks, Troy…for everything."

"No thanks needed. If you decide to do some detective work about Frank Malone or anyone else, let me know. I'd be glad to surf the web with you and see what we can find out."

She frowned. "Maybe we can work on that tomorrow night?"

"That works for me. Just tell me a time to be here. How about I bring Chinese?"

"Nonsense. You aren't going to bring anything but yourself. I make a pretty good sweet-and-sour chicken and fried rice. How does that sound? Shall we say around five?"

"Sounds perfect to me." And with another of his heart-stopping smiles, he was gone.

She closed and locked her front door behind him and then hurried into the kitchen to make sure she had chicken in the freezer for tomorrow night's meal.

There had been a moment that morning when she'd felt like things were moving too fast with Troy. But she didn't know how to slow them down and she wasn't even sure now that she wanted to. She was so conflicted where he was concerned. She had to be so careful because the decisions she made didn't affect just her, but her children as well.

She climbed the stairs to check on Sammy and Katie. They were in Katie's room and had all her dolls seated at the small plastic table. The dolls were adorned in their best dresses and had blingy jewelry dripping from their necks.

"Mommy, I was just going to come down and ask you if we can have a tea party," Katie said.

"I think I can arrange that. It's a little early for lunch, but in an hour or so I'll bring up food for a tea party," Eliza replied. "Now I'm going to work for a little while in my office."

It didn't take long for her to get lost in the big project of building a website for twenty physicians who were a new medical group. She'd been thrilled to get the job and was determined to do the best work possible.

She stayed on task until noon and then stopped to make tea party food. Crusts were cut off peanut butter and jelly sandwiches and she made a quick cucumber-and-tomato salad and set them on a serving tray. She then added fancy cookies she kept for special occasions like this. Finally she made a little teapot full of hot chocolate and carried the tray upstairs.

With the kids taken care of, she continued to work until it was time to make the evening meal. Sammy and Katie had moved downstairs and were watching television in the living room.

She loved the sound of the two giggling together. She hoped they always stayed close and depended on each other for love and whatever else they might need through their lives. She was an only child and had always longed for a sibling.

As she cooked up hamburgers, her thoughts drifted back to the night before and that terrifying moment when she'd believed somebody was in the house.

Had the silhouette she thought she'd seen been a remnant of a dream? Some sort of a nightmare? Or had it been real? Even though she'd been completely certain the night before that the figure was real, she was now leaning toward it being some sort of a figment of her imagination.

The locks on her doors were good ones, and the police had found no evidence of tampering. It had to have just been some sort of a strange, sleep-induced apparition.

One thing was for sure…she was looking forward to an early night. She'd only gotten a couple hours of sleep the night before and she'd fought sleepiness all afternoon.

Dinner was pleasant as Katie and Sammy chatted about the tea party they'd had. "Dolly Isabella ate three cookies," Katie said. "And she didn't use her napkin."

"She was a sloppy pig and very selfish," Sammy said with a giggle. "She drank all the hot chocolate and made the others go without."

"Maybe Dolly Isabella shouldn't be invited to the next tea party," Eliza said, playing along.

"But that would really hurt her feelings," Sammy replied. "We don't want to do that. Maybe we just need to teach her some manners."

For the rest of the meal the conversation revolved around what kind of manners Dolly Isabella needed to learn. It wasn't until after she'd tucked the children into bed that she got back to work in her office.

As the last of the day's sunlight faded, she turned on her desk lamp and then closed the blinds at the window. She loved the fact that her office was in the front of the house where she could gaze out at the sidewalk and street outside during the daytime hours.

However, she always closed the blinds at night when people walking by would have a perfect view into the room. There was no way she wanted anyone seeing the expensive computer and equipment she owned. Open blinds felt like an invitation to any thieves who might wander the streets at night.

Before her brain could really dive into the work she needed to get done, thoughts of Troy intruded. She felt oddly honored that he had trusted her enough to share with her what he'd been through.

Her heart positively wept for the terrible tragedy he'd suffered. She couldn't imagine having a child brutally murdered. It was every parent's worst nightmare.

What really broke her heart was the guilt that Troy obviously carried with him. He blamed himself, but it could have happened to anyone. Eliza didn't know any parent who hadn't taken their eyes off a child for a few moments. It could have happened in a grocery store or in a neighborhood park. It could have happened absolutely anywhere. It was just tragic that in his case evil had been present.

What was even worse was knowing that the man responsible for that heinous murder of a child was free and still walking around and enjoying his life. Justice had definitely let Troy down.

A flush of warmth swept through her as she thought of those moments on his sofa, where she'd almost lost her mind in a haze of blinding desire. It was only the thought of Katie coming down the stairs or Sammy crying out to her that had kept her rational enough to finally call a halt to things between them. But she hadn't wanted it to stop. She'd loved his arms around her as he'd kissed her mindless.

With a shake of her head, she focused on the computer screen before her. Time to get down to work. For the next hour and a half she focused solely on building a website that looked clean and was easy to use.

It was just after ten when she finally scooted away from the desk and rolled her head to relieve the stress in her shoulders.

After the lack of sleep the night before, her bed called to her, but she would have liked to work another hour or two more. But before she got started again she needed to take a break and move around a little bit. She padded into the kitchen, where she made herself a cup of hot tea and grabbed a handful of cookies.

She returned to her office and set the tea and cookies next to her computer, then went to the window and opened a blind to peer outside. From this vantage point she often got a beautiful view of the moon.

Tonight it appeared particularly big and bright. As her gaze drifted downward, every muscle in her body froze. Standing on the sidewalk in front of her house, Leon Whitaker stood staring directly at her.

TROY HAD JUST gotten out of his chair and shut off the television when his cell phone rang. The caller ID showed that it was Eliza.

"Troy." Her voice whispered across the line and he instantly knew something was wrong.

"What is it, Eliza?" he asked urgently.

"He's outside. Leon Whitaker. He's standing outside my house and staring in at me."

"I'll be right out." He hung up and hurried into his bedroom. He opened the drawer next to his bed and pulled out his gun. Unlike the weapon he'd buried in the backyard, this gun was registered to him and felt familiar in his hand.

He'd bought it on the day Annie was born, determined to protect his wife and child from any harm. Ha, what a laugh. Even owning a firearm hadn't protected Annie from evil by the name of Dwight Weatherby.

He stuck the gun in the waist of his jeans and then opened his front door and stepped outside. It was easy to spot the man standing on the sidewalk in front of Eliza's house. A nearby streetlight made it impossible to miss him.

"Can I help you?" Troy asked as he approached.

Leon Whitaker was a tall, thin man with little swords protruding from eyebrow piercings and an ill-kempt mustache that nearly hid his thin upper lip.

"Don't need any help," he replied.

"You're making the woman who lives here very nervous."

Leon grinned. "Good. What are you? Her personal bodyguard?" He looked pointedly at the butt of the gun protruding from Troy's waistband.

"Something like that," Troy replied tersely.

"I just hope I'm making her as nervous as I was last night when the cops showed up at my door. I was in bed with my wife sound asleep when they banged on my door to see if I had broken into this house."

"I imagine the police wouldn't be real happy with you being here now."

Leon laughed, a raspy unpleasant sound. "It's a free country and I'm standing on city property. I'm not breaking any laws here."

Both men turned as Eliza's front door opened and she walked toward them. Her shoulders were squared and her chin was raised as if anticipating a fight. She looked beautiful with her hair loose and blowing in the wind that had picked up earlier in the evening.

When she reached where they stood, she looked at Leon. "Were you in my house last night?"

"I was not, and I didn't appreciate you siccing the

cops on me," he replied with an upthrust of his chin. "In my line of work I don't want to draw any police attention. I wasn't in your damned house and you had no right to put my name in your mouth with the police."

"I'm sorry, but what else was I to think since you've been harassing me with your text messages and nasty emails? I don't owe you anything, Leon. I thought we parted ways amicably," she said. Even under stress, she looked beautiful with the moonlight playing on her delicate features.

"You ticked me off," Leon replied. "I know how good you are at what you do and I wanted you to do a kick-ass website for me."

"And I'm sorry that I couldn't do that for you and I explained why. Please stop the harassment, Leon. I'm sure you found somebody else to work for you on the web pages."

Troy wanted to beat the living daylights out of the man who would harass a woman the way this creep had done to Eliza. What kind of a man did something like that to a woman?

"I did find somebody else, somebody who isn't so uptight with their morals," Leon replied.

"Then please just leave me alone," Eliza said.

Leon stared at her for a long moment and then slowly nodded his head. "Okay, I'll stop with the texts and emails, but you have to agree to keep my name out of your mouth when it comes to the cops. I wasn't in your house last night and I have no intention of ever being in your house." He grinned. "Besides, harassing you has been pretty boring since you never answer me."

"So we have a deal? You'll stop harassing me and I won't ever mention you to the police again?"

"We have a deal," he replied.

"Thank you," Eliza said, her relief evident in her tone of voice.

Leon gave a final nod and then turned and headed down the sidewalk to where a car was parked at the curb. Eliza turned and gazed at Troy. "It seems like I'm always telling you thank you," she said.

"You're welcome," he replied. "Do you believe he's done and is going to leave you alone now?"

"God, I hope so. But I do believe that he wasn't in my house last night. The person I thought I saw appeared heavier than Leon." She released a deep sigh. "I'm leaning toward believing nobody was in the house and it was just some strange dream or night terror."

"All I know is that you did the right thing getting the children out and running to my place," he replied.

"Speaking of…" She glanced toward her front door. "I need to get back inside."

"Are we still on for tomorrow night?"

"Absolutely," she replied. "No matter what's going on, I wouldn't mind learning something about Frank Malone, especially given the hidey-holes we've found in the house."

"Then I'll see you tomorrow evening," he replied. "Go ahead and get inside."

He watched until she disappeared back into the house and then he checked the street; Leon's car was also gone. Stupid creep, he thought derisively as he began the walk across the lawn to his own place.

He was just about to his own front door when he thought he saw a figure dart around the side of his house. Instantly adrenaline cranked up inside him and his heartbeat raced a frantic rhythm in his chest.

Grabbing the gun from his waistband, he gripped it firmly in his hand and moved toward the corner of the house. Had Leon parked just out of sight and returned for more mischief?

He reached the corner, and drawing a quick breath, he whirled around it. Nobody was on the side of the house.

The hot night air wrapped around him, oppressive and heavy, making it difficult for him to draw a full breath. The breeze that had stirred the air only moments before was gone. Sweat began to bead on his forehead.

He walked the length of the house to the next corner and when he reached it, he once again stepped around it, giving him a full moonlit view of his backyard.

Nobody. He lowered the gun and expelled a deep breath. He could have sworn he'd seen somebody creeping around in the shadows of the night.

At the back edge of the yard was a wooded area where occasionally deer wandered. Were those trees now hiding something more ominous?

He stood for several long moments, his gaze shooting from left to right. Had he only imagined the figure? He couldn't be sure.

As he remained staring into the woods, he remembered his conversation with Nick. Of the six men who had entered the murder pact, he was fairly certain that one of them had gone rogue and he was killing the targets himself in a horrific way.

That meant there were five men on the face of the earth who could identify and turn him in. Liabilities. Loose ends. Despite the heat of the night, a faint chill worked up his spine.

Maybe it was time for him to watch his own back as well as watching Eliza's.

Chapter Six

It had been a pleasure that morning for Eliza to open up her email and text messages and have no nasty ones from Leon Whitaker. Maybe he'd really meant it the night before when he'd told her he was done tormenting her.

They had just gotten back from church service when her phone rang. The caller ID let her know who it was and she quickly answered.

"Hi, Lucy," she said.

"Hey, Eliza. How's it going?"

"It's going. How about you?"

"Same, but I think it's time for me to borrow your kids for a night. I'm having Katie and Sammy withdrawal."

Eliza laughed. "Well, you know they love it when you borrow them."

"I was thinking next Friday night. I'll take them out for dinner and then bring them home Saturday morning after I make them breakfast. Would that work for you?"

"Sounds good to me," Eliza replied.

"Great, then I'll see you on Friday."

The two hung up and Eliza sat back in her office chair, where she'd been since getting home from church. The kids would be delighted, and Lucy White was the only person on the face of the earth she would trust them with for an overnight stay.

Lucy was forty-one years old, unmarried, and worked as an aide at Sammy's school. She and Sammy had bonded immediately and it wasn't long before Lucy had become a grandmother-like figure to the kids. They loved slumber partying at Lucy's house and she loved having them.

It would be a night with no children for Eliza. Should she tell Troy? A shiver of pleasure washed over her. If she told him and they got together, she was fairly certain they would make love that night.

Was she ready for that? Her lips definitely yearned for more of his kisses and her body longed for his touch, but her brain overrode those feelings with questions and a faint wariness.

Troy certainly hadn't claimed undying love for her and if he had, she wouldn't have believed him. It was far too soon to be thinking about love with him.

They hadn't known each other long and yet she felt as if she'd known him for months.

She'd never been the kind of woman to just fall into bed with a man. She'd only had one lover before she'd married Blake and that had been her high school sweetheart, whom she had dated for four years.

So if she slept with Troy there would be no promise of commitment. There wouldn't even be an assurance that they would see each other again in a dating capacity. Could she live with that? She didn't know. All she did know was it was time to get busy making the evening meal.

Before she could get started, the doorbell rang. She opened the door to a fiftysomething man. His dark brown uniform shirt pulled taut around his bulky upper arms and his uniform pants appeared to be about an inch or so too short. An emblem on the shirt pocket was that of the electric company.

"Good afternoon, ma'am," he said. He smiled, but the gesture didn't quite reach the darkness of his eyes. "Are you Eliza Burke?"

"Yes, I am. May I help you?" she asked, oddly grateful there was a locked screen door between them.

"Sorry to bother you on this fine afternoon, but your electric meter has stopped registering correctly and I need to come inside and check out some of your wiring."

She looked past him to the white panel van that was parked in her driveway. There were no markings identifying the van as belonging to any company. That, coupled with his slightly ill-kempt appearance, caused little alarm bells to ring loudly in her head.

"Can I see some kind of identification?" she asked.

He pulled a frayed black wallet out of his back pocket and flipped it open and showed it to her. It appeared to be a legitimate Kansas City Power and Light photo identification.

According to the ID his name was Max Sampson and he'd been a KCPL worker for the past five years. Still, her sense of unease wasn't allayed. She, more than most people, with her experience on the web, knew how easy it was to make and laminate a badge or an identification card that would look realistic. Besides, she'd never heard of an electric company working on Sundays unless it was an emergency. Her power was working just fine so there was definitely no emergency.

"Now, can I come in and get to work?" he asked as he re-pocketed his wallet.

"I'm sorry. I'm having a dinner party and my guests will be arriving anytime. Now isn't convenient for me. Could you have somebody call me to-morrow to set up an appointment?"

He frowned. "I wouldn't interfere with your dinner party."

"I would prefer we don't do this now," she replied.

His frown deepened. "You could go ahead and make the appointment with me right now."

"I'm sorry, but this really isn't convenient for me right now," she repeated more firmly. "Just have somebody call me tomorrow." She closed the door and locked it, her heart beating a slightly accelerated rhythm.

She moved from the door to the window and released a sigh of relief as she watched him walk across the lawn to his van. She continued to watch as he backed out of the driveway and then disappeared down the block.

She wasn't sure why, but all her instincts had been to keep him out of the house. He'd been wearing the right uniform and had what appeared to be proper identification, but that hadn't mattered. Something had felt off and she never ignored her gut instinct.

She immediately went into her office and to her computer, where she pulled up the home page for Kansas City Power and Light. She called the contact number the web page displayed.

After four rings a woman answered and identified herself as Jennifer Belvin. Eliza explained the situation and when she was finished there was a long moment of silence.

"Are you sure he was from Kansas City Power and Light?" Jennifer finally asked.

"That's what he said. He was wearing a dark brown uniform and he had an identification card with the KCPL logo on it."

"Did you call for service?"

"No," Eliza replied. "As far as I'm concerned everything in my home has been working just fine."

"If it was a meter issue there's no reason for the technician to come into your house. The meter is outside," Jennifer replied. "Please just give me a minute to check a few things."

"Thank you." As Eliza waited to the sound of some unidentifiable music, a fluttery fear once again rose up inside her.

She tried to calm herself. Maybe it was just some sort of a crazy mistake. Perhaps Max Sampson had the address wrong. Surely these kinds of things happened occasionally.

And yet he'd known her name.

"Ma'am?" Jennifer came back on the line.

"Yes, I'm here," Eliza replied.

"We have no record of any problems with your meter and we didn't send a technician to your home.

If I were you I might think about calling the police, and I'll make a note of this issue here."

"Thank you." Eliza hung up and moved to the window, the fear moving up the back of her throat and squeezing tight. There was no sign of the white van, but that certainly didn't ease her concern.

She doubted that the man's name was really Max Sampson. So who was he and what had he really wanted? Why had he wanted to come into her house?

There was no reason for the police to come to her house. She had no idea where the man in the white van had gone, but she definitely wanted to make a report of what had just happened.

It was possible the man was some kind of a predator with a list of single women's names and addresses in his pocket. If he had gained entry would he have robbed her? Raped her?

Her heart nearly stopped as she thought of her babies upstairs. What would he do with them if he'd gotten inside? A chill of horror worked up her spine.

Would somebody call her tomorrow and set up an appointment? If anyone called, she wouldn't believe they were who they claimed to be. There was no way she was opening her door tomorrow or any other day to a "technician" from the electric company.

Instead of calling 911, she got on the computer and found out the phone number to the nearest police station. She was in no imminent danger and didn't want to tie up an emergency operator.

After she made the report, she climbed the stairs, suddenly needing to see Katie and Sammy. They were in Sammy's room playing with miniature cars.

"I have the police car and I had to give Sammy a ticket for speeding," Katie said with a giggle.

Eliza fought the impulse to grab both of her kids and give each of them the biggest hug in the world. But they were laughing and having fun and she didn't want them to feel any of the negative tension that still roared through her.

"Remember when you got a speeding ticket, Mommy?" Sammy asked.

"You were mad," Katie said.

"I was mad at myself, not the police officer who gave me the ticket. Speeding is a bad thing to do. You should always drive under the speed limit," she replied. "And now I'm going to get busy cooking dinner."

"And Mr. Troy is coming over," Katie replied. She and her brother clapped their hands together, obviously happy to share dinner with their favorite neighbor.

Before heading into the kitchen, Eliza went back downstairs and to the front window. She gazed up and down the street, looking for the white panel van, but she saw nothing to cause her alarm. Still, as she got started on the cooking, she occasionally wandered back to the front window just to check. At one point a police car drove by and she was grateful that they were in the area.

As she worked on the sweet-and-sour chicken she had promised Troy, her thoughts turned to the mission for the night. She was almost afraid of what they might find out about Frank Malone.

The more she thought about it the more she realized Blake hadn't told her too much about the grandfather who had raised him. She knew that Frank and his wife had divorced when Blake was nine and he'd never seen his grandmother again.

Eliza had spent time with Frank twice early in her marriage and both times he'd seemed like an affable old man who had entertained them over dinner with stories about Blake's childhood.

She wasn't sure what she feared finding out. The house had felt like such a gift when she'd learned it had been left to her. She just hoped it didn't turn out to be some sort of a curse.

The meal was ready to serve at five o'clock when Troy arrived. "This looks great," he said when she set his plate in front of him.

"We like Mommy's sweet-and-sour better than Mr. Chow's," Katie said, referencing a nearby restaurant.

"I like the pineapple pieces best of all," Sammy added.

Troy smiled at her. "You definitely have a fan club here."

She laughed. "They know where their bread is buttered." As always when she was around him, little butterflies danced in her stomach. He looked so handsome seated across the table from her with his blue-striped shirt enhancing the blue of his eyes.

Even more attractive was how normal it felt for him to be seated at the table and chatting with the children. It was obvious the kids adored him and Eliza could definitely get used to him being here all the time.

Too fast, she reminded herself. She was thinking about a future that had nothing to do with reality. She didn't even know if Troy was interested in any kind of a long-term relationship with her.

She hadn't intended on dating while Katie and Sammy were young, but Troy had appeared out of nowhere. His presence made her realize how hungry she was for a relationship and how she ached to be loved. She had never truly felt that way during her marriage. She'd also like it if her children would have a loving, supportive male figure in their lives.

However, she had to tread carefully with Troy. She would hate to fall into a relationship with him when she wasn't ready or they both weren't on the same page. She would definitely hate to lose him as a valued and caring neighbor, and it would be far too easy to have a failed relationship with him that made it impossible for them to even remain friends. That was the last thing she wanted to happen.

Dinner conversation revolved around school, the kids' friends, and all the manners they were teaching Dolly Isabella. Troy began to make up goofy manners, making them all laugh.

"That was one of the best meals I've ever eaten," he said later as they cleared the dishes. The kids had gone into the living room for some television time, after which it would be bath and bedtime for them.

"Thanks. I do enjoy cooking."

"It shows," he replied.

"Coffee?" she asked.

"That sounds good," he replied.

She fixed the coffee and then joined him at the table. "You definitely entertained us throughout the meal."

He grinned. "I was a bit silly, but it's fun to make the kids laugh."

"They can be pretty goofy themselves," she replied, then sobered. "Something strange happened today."

"What's that?" One of his dark eyebrows quirked upward.

As she told him about the man who had pretended to be a KCPL worker, his eyes darkened. "Thank God you followed your instincts and didn't let him in," he said when she'd finished. "Did you call the police?"

"I did. They took an official report over the phone and told me it might have been an attempt at some kind of a home invasion or robbery. The officer I spoke to said the bad guys are getting more and more innovative when it comes to committing their crimes."

"Terrific," he replied drily. "Just what we need… criminals getting smarter."

"Hopefully the police are keeping an eye out for this guy so he won't get a chance to prey on anyone else." She fought against a chill that suddenly threatened to walk up her spine.

"I'm sure there's probably a patrol car in the area keeping an eye out," he replied. "So, are you ready to see what we can find out about the man who left you this house?" he asked.

She took a sip of her coffee and then set down

her cup. "To be honest, I'm almost afraid of what we might find out. Maybe he was a big crime lord back in the day. Or maybe he was some kind of a serial killer and there are ghosts of dead people roaming around in here at night." She released a small laugh at his look of stunned surprise. "Okay, tell me I'm crazy."

He smiled. "I wouldn't say you're crazy, but I definitely will say you have a big imagination." He wrapped his hands around his coffee cup. "Do you believe in ghosts?"

She frowned thoughtfully and leaned back in her chair. "I'm not sure what I believe when it comes to all the paranormal stuff. All I know for sure is that if this house has ghosts, then they are darned noisy ones."

She picked up her coffee cup once again. A sense of inexplicable dread coursed through her. "Shall we head into my office and see if we can find where the dead bodies are buried?"

ELIZA SAT IN her office chair and Troy sat right next to her in a straight-backed one he'd brought from the kitchen. As always when he was near her the scent of her stirred him, creating an itch inside him he wanted her to scratch.

What surprised him as much as anything was that

his attraction to her wasn't just a sexual one, although that was certainly strong. He also loved the sound of her laughter and how easily she laughed.

He admired the work ethic that had financially taken care of her and her two children when her marriage had fallen apart. He especially liked the fierce love she had for her children and wondered what it would be like to be loved that way.

He'd loved his wife, and he believed she'd loved him, but when he'd needed her the most she'd turned her back on him. There had been no love, no forgiveness at all in her heart for him. She'd blamed him for their daughter's murder and her love had turned to hate for him.

Sherry had been hurting as deeply as he had, but instead of getting through it together, she'd chosen to blame and hate.

"So, tell me more about your fear of ghosts," he said once they were settled in. He needed something to take away his thoughts of the past. "Are you also afraid to walk in a cemetery after dark? Do you hold your breath when a hearse goes by?"

"Now you're making fun of me," she replied with a twinkle in her eyes.

"Maybe just a little." He took a sip of his coffee. "What are you really afraid of, Eliza Burke?"

She leaned back in the chair and looked at him

thoughtfully. "I'm afraid I'll die while my children still need me. I'm afraid something will happen and I won't be able to support them. And cats... I'm deathly afraid of cats."

"Really? Cats?" He looked at her in surprise. "I thought all women liked cats."

"Not this woman. I was traumatized by my grandmother's cat every time I went to visit her. Sweetkins was a loving kitty according to my grandma, but I thought she was a demon from the very depths of hell. She spent the entire time I was at my grandma's house hiding and then jumping out at me when I least expected it. Grandma would tell me she wanted to play, but I was terrified of little Sweetkins."

He laughed, delighted by the small glimpse into her childhood. "So, you were close to your grandmother?"

"Yes. She was my grandmother on my father's side and she and my grandpa lived on a farm in western Kansas. Every summer I'd spend a couple of weeks with them. Grandma would take me out to pick tomatoes or green beans and my grandpa would let me ride on the tractor with him. It always felt like an adventure being with them."

"That's nice. I didn't know my grandparents," he replied. "They were all already gone when I was born."

"That's sad."

"That's life," he replied with a small shrug.

"So, Mr. Troy Anderson, tell me what you're afraid of," she said. She picked up her coffee cup and her beautiful eyes gazed at him curiously as she looked at him over the brim.

He couldn't tell her that he feared a grief-stricken man had gone off the rails and now might want him and four other men dead. He couldn't share anything about the murder pact he'd made while he'd been in the very depths of hell.

He also wasn't willing to share with her that he was terrified of loving again. He was enjoying their relationship, but certainly didn't intend to put his heart on the line ever again.

"I've already lived my worst fear," he finally replied. "So now I'm not afraid of much of anything." He cleared his throat as emotion attempted to rise up in him.

She reached out and covered his hand with hers on the top of the desk. That simple touch warmed the ice that had threatened to consume him. She had pretty hands with slender fingers and nails painted a pastel pink. They were warm and seemed to transmit comfort.

For a moment neither of them spoke. Finally it was he who found his voice once again. "So, any word from Leon the creep?" he asked.

"No, thankfully." She removed her hand from his.

"I imagine he decided to fly right once the police visited his house."

She gave him a wry smile. "Your showing up with a gun might have had something to do with his sudden change of heart."

"Thank God I didn't have to actually use it. It's been packed away in my bedroom nightstand for several years and there weren't even any bullets in it."

She laughed, that full-bodied sound that he loved to hear. "So you were all bluster and no bite."

"If he would have touched you in any way, you would have definitely seen my bite," he replied. For a moment their gazes locked. Oh, how easily he could fall into the soft gray depths of her eyes.

She cleared her throat and broke the gaze. "Let's get this started." He leaned toward her as she typed Frank Malone's name into the search bar. The screen filled with hits. Frank Malone was a lawyer in Seattle, Washington. He was a blues singer in Tennessee. He was the mayor of a small town in Maine.

She shook her head. "That was silly of me. Obviously I need to narrow the search to Kansas City." Her slender fingers flew over the keyboard once again.

This time there were fewer results. "I'd say we

can agree that the Frank Malone we're looking for isn't on Twitter," he said.

She laughed. "We can definitely agree on that." She scrolled down farther. "And we can also agree that he isn't an exotic dancer willing to entertain at private parties."

"I'm surprised an obituary didn't pop up."

She frowned. "Now that you mention it, I don't remember seeing one. I didn't even know he had died until the lawyer contacted me about the house. The lawyer did tell me he was cremated."

"Have you ever used the site KCPersons.com?"

"No, I've never heard of it," she replied. She shifted positions in the chair and once again her heady scent surrounded him.

"It's a site that has bios and information about the notable people in Kansas City. And by notable I mean the famous and the infamous."

"I doubt that Frank was considered a notable person."

"Maybe it's worth looking at," he replied. "Although I have to admit the information there isn't vetted properly at all. They have me listed as being fifty-five years old. They're exactly twenty years off my real age."

She raised an eyebrow. "You're listed as one of Kansas City's notable persons?"

He shook his head. "I don't know how I got listed on the site, but I'm guessing it had something to do with an article that appeared in the *Kansas City Star* newspaper where local businesses and services were highlighted."

"How did you know you were on the site?"

He cast her a slightly sheepish grin. "I Google myself occasionally. Actually, I do it to make sure there aren't any disgruntled customers out there talking negatively about me or the business."

"Have you ever found any?"

"Three. Over the years I've only had three customers complain about my service. In two of those cases I contacted the people and made things right with them."

"And in the third case?"

"She was a diva. Short of offering her my services free for the rest of her life, she wasn't going to be happy. Now, enough about me, let's see if Frank Malone made the Kansas City notable site."

Once again, her fingers quickly tapped over the keys. "Wow, I can't believe I didn't know about this," she said when the site opened up. There was a search bar in the upper right-hand corner and she typed in Frank's name.

"He's here," she said in surprise.

"It looks like he was added two weeks ago," Troy observed.

"So somebody wrote this bio after his death."

They both leaned forward to read. The first part of the bio was about where Frank Malone was born and went to school. It appeared to be a fairly unremarkable life until he was seventeen, at which time he was convicted of the robbery of a video store. He spent time in juvenile detention and was released just after his eighteenth birthday. He was in trouble again when he was twenty-two, this time convicted of robbing a convenience store.

"He definitely wasn't a Boy Scout when he was young," Troy said as she moved the cursor to pull up the next page.

He could feel Eliza's tension. It wafted from her as strongly as her scent. For the life of him, he couldn't figure out what kind of information they'd learn about Frank Malone that would have anything to do with her or the house the man had left to her.

The second page of the bio was devoted to his marriage and more legal trouble culminating fifteen years earlier when he and three other men were prime suspects in what the news reports had called the Great Flake Jewel Heist. The other men were named, but none of them went to trial due to a lack of evidence. The bio ended with his death.

She turned to look at Troy. "I guess we need to look up the Great Flake Jewel Heist and find out what that was all about."

"Go for it," he agreed, intrigued by what they'd find.

"I know Flake Jewelry is a high-end store here in town, but I don't remember a big robbery ever taking place there," she said as she typed in the appropriate words.

"Would you have paid any attention to a news report about it fifteen years ago?"

She shook her head. "Probably not."

Her search yielded several results and she punched on the first one. It detailed the robbery of the store, which had occurred at night. Various pieces of jewelry were stolen, but the biggest loss was of a necklace that had been on loan from a jewelry store in Paris, a necklace worth $2.4 million.

"Well, the good news is I don't think Frank was a serial killer, but it's very possible he was a jewel thief," Troy said.

"I want to see what I can find out about the other men listed as potential suspects in the jewelry robbery."

She went back to the bio and wrote down the three names listed there. "We'll start with Lester Cantano. At least his name isn't common."

Dear Reader,

IT'S A FACT: if you answer 4 quick questions, we'll send you **4 FREE REWARDS!**

I'm not kidding you. As a leading publisher of women's fiction, we value your opinions… and your time. That's why we are prepared to **reward** you handsomely for completing our mini-survey. In fact, we have 4 Free Rewards for you, including 2 free books and 2 free gifts.

As you may have guessed, that's why our mini-survey is called **"4 for 4".** Answer 4 questions and get 4 Free Rewards. It's that simple!

Thank you for participating in our survey,

Pam Powers

To get your 4 FREE REWARDS:
Complete the survey below and return the insert today to receive 2 FREE BOOKS and 2 FREE GIFTS guaranteed!

"4 for 4" MINI-SURVEY

1 Is reading one of your favorite hobbies?
☐ YES ☐ NO

2 Do you prefer to read instead of watch TV?
☐ YES ☐ NO

3 Do you read newspapers and magazines?
☐ YES ☐ NO

4 Do you enjoy trying new book series with FREE BOOKS?
☐ YES ☐ NO

YES! I have completed the above Mini-Survey. Please send me my 4 FREE REWARDS (worth over $20 retail). I understand that I am under no obligation to buy anything, as explained on the back of this card.

☐ I prefer the regular-print edition
182/382 HDL GNQ7

☐ I prefer the larger-print edition
199/399 HDL GNQ7

FIRST NAME	LAST NAME

ADDRESS

APT.#	CITY

STATE/PROV.	ZIP/POSTAL CODE

An obituary with a picture of the man appeared. "He died five years ago," Eliza said aloud.

"What about Neil Riddicio?"

"Look, he has a social media page."

Neil's profile photo showed him to be a tough-looking sixty-year-old guy. It listed him as being an IT expert who also enjoyed powerful motorcycles and bar fights.

"Not exactly a pillar of society," Troy said drily.

"I still can't figure out what any of this might have to do with me or this house," she replied. "Let's see what we can find out about Mitchell Martinson. Oh, good. He's on social media, too."

She pulled up the site and then gasped in obvious horror and pulled her fingers off the keyboard. "That's Max." Her voice trembled as her face paled.

Troy looked at the photo of the scruffy, dark-haired man and then gazed back at Eliza. "Max who?" he asked in confusion.

"Max…he was the man who came here earlier and pretended to be from the power company."

The man had pretended to be an electric technician to get into the house. Why? They had to figure out what the hell was going on. All of a sudden he didn't smell Eliza's enchanting scent or feel the warmth of her body close to his.

All he smelled, all he felt at the moment, was a tight twist of his gut as a dark cloud of danger descended over her.

Chapter Seven

"Mommy?"

Eliza jumped at the sound of Katie's voice. Bitter fear lingered in her mouth and she forced a smile to her face. "Yes, honey." She was grateful her voice held none of the panic that pulsed inside her.

"Sammy fell asleep on the sofa and I'm ready for bed, too." Katie rubbed her eyes with her fists, a gesture she always did when she was overtired.

Eliza looked at the clock on her wall and nearly gasped. It was definitely past their bedtimes. "We'll skip baths for tonight," she said. "Go get into your jammies and I'll be up to tuck you in."

"I want Mr. Troy to tuck me in," Katie said.

"I think I can do that," Troy replied. "In fact, I'll carry Sammy up." Eliza looked at him gratefully. They both got up from the desk.

Troy carried a still-sleeping Sammy up to his bed and Eliza went with Katie to get her ready for sleep

time. All the while the information she and Troy
had gleaned about Frank Malone whirled around
and around in her head. A jewel thief? Was it really possible?

And the fact that Max had pretended to be a utility worker to gain access inside her house made everything even more horrifying.

Katie crawled into bed and by that time Troy appeared in her doorway. "All ready for a Mr. Troy
tuck-in?" he asked.

"Yes," Katie replied.

Troy walked across the room and sat on the edge
of her bed. He reached out and moved a strand of her
hair away from her little face. "May the light of the
moon and the stars guide you into the land of happy
dreams." He leaned over and pecked her on the cheek.
"Sleep tight and don't let the bedbugs bite."

Katie giggled. "Mommy says that sometimes,
too. Good night, Mr. Troy." She grabbed her favorite stuffed bear to her chest and was asleep almost
immediately.

Eliza looked in on Sammy, grateful to see that
Troy had taken off his shoes and covered him with
the sheet. She moved his shoes from the side of the
bed to the foot of the bed where Sammy was accustomed to finding them. Then she and Troy went back
down the stairs.

Instead of leading him back into the office, she went into the living room and sat on the edge of the sofa. He sank down next to her.

"That was a beautiful tuck-in," she said.

"Thanks. It's what my mother used to say to me at bedtime."

"Where are your parents? You've never mentioned them to me."

"They divorced when I was eight. My father passed away six years ago from a heart attack. My mother remarried and moved to France when I turned eighteen. She didn't stay in touch with my dad or me after that."

"That's terrible. I'm so sorry," she replied. He hadn't even had his parents' support when tragedy had fractured his entire life.

He shrugged. "To be honest, she wasn't much of a mother even when she was present in my life. But that's enough about me. What are you thinking about what we just learned?" he asked.

She released a small laugh. "My brain is positively spinning in my head and I'm thinking of a million things all at the same time."

He cast her a gentle smile that only added to the emotions rushing through her. At least the smile offered her his support, and that helped her deal with all the negative thoughts.

He leaned back in the sofa. "So, you had no clue

that your husband's grandfather was a lifelong criminal?"

"None. That's something Blake didn't ever say anything about," she replied.

"I can see why Blake might not mention it. You said the two men weren't that close. Blake was probably embarrassed by his convict grandfather."

"You could be right about that," she replied with a sigh. "Shall we talk about the elephant in the room? The fact that he was a suspect in a big jewel theft?"

"And the jewels were never recovered," Troy replied.

An icy chill washed over her at those words. "But he was just a suspect," she said in an effort to somehow comfort herself. "He wasn't even officially charged with the crime. That means it's very possible he didn't do it."

"And yet you had one of his thug friends, a fellow suspect, show up today wanting to get inside the house," he countered. "We have to consider that it's possible the jewels are hidden someplace here in the house."

She fought back a gasp even though she'd known that was where the conversation would lead. "I certainly don't know where. We've found a couple of hidey-holes but they've been empty."

"Then maybe you just haven't found the right hidey-holes," he replied.

"I find it hard to believe the jewels are in the house considering that this crime happened over fifteen years ago. Wouldn't the thieves have already fenced them or whatever? Why steal jewels and just stick them in a hidey-hole in the wall for fifteen years?"

Troy frowned. "I certainly don't know how these things work, but I would guess it was fairly easy to get rid of some of the smaller pieces of stolen jewelry when the theft occurred, but that $2.4 million necklace would be much more difficult."

"I just feel so overwhelmed right now," she admitted.

He reached out and took her hand in his. "You aren't alone in this, Eliza. I'll do whatever I can to help you."

She squeezed his hand. "Thank you, but I'm not sure what kind of help I need. Should I call the police?"

"If that would make you feel better, then definitely you should make that call. But I'm afraid there's not much they would be able to do. We're just speculating on a possibility right now."

"It was obvious Max wanted inside the house, so he must believe something of value is in here." At the moment her home, the place she should feel the safest, instead felt like a place of danger. She looked at Troy helplessly. "What should I do?" she whispered.

He threw an arm around her shoulder and pulled her closer to his side. "If I were you, the first thing I would do is get an alarm system…as in tomorrow if it's possible. If getting one is an issue due to finances, then I'll help you with it."

"Thank you, but that's not necessary." She couldn't believe he was so nice as to offer financial help if she needed it. "I'll call somebody first thing in the morning and get that taken care of." She would make sure every door and window was covered with bells and whistles should somebody try to make their way inside. As she remembered that night when she was sure there had been somebody in the house, an intense shiver raised goose bumps on her arms. Yes, she definitely wanted an alarm system sooner rather than later. "Then what?"

"We search to find out what secrets this house might still hold."

She leaned against him. She'd always considered herself to be a strong woman, but at the moment she felt lost and afraid. "I can't exactly tear up the floor and walls with a blind child in the house. I don't even want my children to know anything about this. The last thing I want is to do anything that upsets their routine or makes them be afraid."

"I understand that, but there's no reason why you and I can't do a search of this place and look for more hidey-holes while the kids are in school. They found a couple without tearing up the house."

"That sounds like a plan," she replied. She sat up, feeling stronger with a definite plan in place. She got up and walked over to the place where Sammy had found the newest hidey-hole. Troy watched her curiously as she ran her fingers along the wainscoting. When she felt an irregularity in the wood, she pushed on it and the hidden door popped open. "This is the newest one Sammy found."

Troy's eyes widened and he got up off the sofa and joined her in front of the large space. "Looks like a great place to hide if the police came into the house."

"And the secret stairway Sammy found would also help somebody get from upstairs to downstairs without anyone being the wiser," she said. Knowing Frank's history suddenly made the hidey-holes in the house make more sense.

Were there jewels still hidden in the house? Was that what Max aka Mitchell was looking for after all this time? And if that was the case, what kind of danger were she and the children in? A shudder of fear swept through her.

Troy must have seen it for he pulled her into his arms. She leaned against him, loving his warmth and the unspoken support he offered her. Again she wondered, how had she gotten so lucky to have him as a neighbor?

Who was she kidding…he was becoming much more than just a helpful neighbor to her. She was precariously close to being in love with him and that thought both thrilled her and filled her with just a little bit of fear, because she had no idea where he was at with her.

Her feelings toward him had blossomed so fast she wasn't sure she could trust them. Would she have been vulnerable to any man who showed her attention and support as she went through this disturbing time and with so many mysteries floating in the air? She honestly didn't know the answer.

She lowered her head to the crook of his neck and breathed in the scent of him. His arms tightened around her. "Make sure you get that alarm installed first thing tomorrow," he said.

"Definitely first thing in the morning," she agreed. She raised her head and looked at him as her heart began to beat an unsteady rhythm. "My children are going to be gone all night next Friday night. I was wondering if you'd like to come over for dinner."

His eyes lit with small flames as his hands moved

up and down her back. "I've got a better deal for you. You've already cooked several meals for me—how about next Friday night you come to my place and I'll provide the meal?"

"Okay, then I'll bring dessert," she said, half-breathless by the heat in his eyes.

"You can be dessert."

She released a small, unsteady laugh and he dropped his arms from around her and stepped back. "It's getting late. Will you be okay here tonight?"

"We'll be fine." She was grateful he was calling an end to the night. Her head was not only spinning with the information about Frank and a jewel heist, but also with the knowledge that she'd effectively set up a night of lovemaking with Troy.

She knew that's what would happen. There was no doubt in her mind that Friday they would take their relationship to the next level.

They headed for the front door. "I'll come over tomorrow afternoon so we can start our search for more hiding places," he said.

"I feel like I'm taking up all your free time," she replied. "And work time...don't you usually work in the afternoons?"

"If I minded, I wouldn't have made the offer to help, and when you're the boss you get to pick your own hours." He flashed her the smile that always shot a delicious warmth through her. "I'll see you tomorrow afternoon unless something else happens that frightens you and then you know I'm only a phone call away."

He pressed his lips against her forehead in a gentle kiss and then opened the front door. "Get some sleep, Eliza. I know it's been a long day for you."

Suddenly she was exhausted. It seemed like she hadn't gotten a good night's sleep since she'd moved into this house over a month ago. "Good night, Troy. I'll see you tomorrow."

When he was gone she wandered around the living room, her gaze drifting from wall to wall. Was it really possible there were priceless jewels hidden someplace in the walls? If so, why would Frank not do something with them after all this time? If four men had robbed a jewelry store, then why hadn't they sold the goods and split the profits?

Was it possible the men had agreed to wait? That the necklace was just too hot, too big to get rid of right away? Had they made a deal to wait a certain number of years before trying to get rid of it? Had Frank's death changed everything?

Mitchell had wanted to come in and "look at her wiring." There could be only one reason he'd want to do that and that was because he believed there was something hidden in her walls. Perhaps the necklace worth millions of dollars? What measures would the man go to in order to reach his goal? The possibilities of what he might do chilled her to the very bone.

She turned out the lights and took a final look outside. There was nothing out there to cause her pause. Still, she couldn't wait until morning so she could arrange for a security system. Then and only then would she feel completely safe in her own home.

She went upstairs, checked on each of her children and then went into her own bedroom and got ready for bed. Her thoughts shifted to Troy.

What had she done? By telling Troy her children would be gone next Friday night she'd basically told him she'd sleep with him that night.

Was she really ready for that? Would it move her and Troy into a deeper, more meaningful relationship or would he cool things off after having gotten what he wanted? And there was no doubt in her mind that he wanted her.

She felt his desire for her every time they were together. It shone from his eyes and radiated in the simplest touch from him. Was he just looking for an easy conquest?

Mystery and the potential of danger surrounded her, but the idea of finding out Troy might not be the wonderful man she believed him to be was almost as frightening.

TROY WAS RIDICULOUSLY pleased when he left his house early the next morning that a white panel van with the logo of Home Security Done Right was in Eliza's driveway.

He'd heard good things about that particular home alarm company and he would definitely sleep far better at night knowing she and the children were protected from intruders by a security system. He certainly hadn't gotten much sleep the night before.

The idea of jewels from a fifteen-year-old heist being hidden in her house seemed more than a bit far-fetched. And yet he couldn't figure out any other reason for the things that had taken place. The most telling was the fact that Mitchell, a man who had been named as a suspect in that long-ago heist, had shown up on her front porch wanting to get inside.

If Frank and the men had really stolen those jewels, then what kind of a deal had they made to reap the benefits? Was it possible the jewels had been in the house all along and Frank's death had somehow changed the plans?

Those thoughts weren't the only ones that had kept him tossing and turning all through the night. The physical chemistry between him and Eliza was definitely off the charts.

When she told him the children wouldn't be home on Friday night there had been a promise in her eyes, a promise that had instantly shot white-hot desire through him.

He hoped to finish up his day by around one, which would give him and Eliza a couple hours to look for more hidey-holes in the house while the children were still in school.

If there were any jewels inside, he and Eliza would find them and turn them over to the police. Hopefully a news report would confirm to everyone that the jewels had been found, and any bad guys who wanted to search for them would just go away.

Today he was checking in on all his working crews to make sure things were going smoothly. When summer and fall were over his work didn't end. He switched out his lawn mowers for snow blowers and his trucks would sport snow blades. He had several contracts with neighborhood associations to keep their roads cleared and sidewalks clean after a snowfall.

The morning passed quickly with him driving from job to job and checking in. For the most part the people who worked for him were hard workers who knew he expected them to adhere to his high standards. He paid well and considered himself a fair boss. He felt as if all his workers respected him, and he respected them as well.

It was one thirty when he landed at Eliza's house.

She greeted him with a big smile. "The alarm company just left," she said as she ushered him into the kitchen. "I now have enough bells and whistles in here to keep out anyone."

"That definitely makes me feel better," he replied.

"Me, too. I even have a master panel in my bedroom that will show me, if there is a breach, exactly where in the house it occurred."

"That sounds perfect." And she looked better than perfect. Clad in a pair of white jean shorts and a mint-green blouse and with her hair pulled up in a ponytail, she looked fresh and lovely and as if a weight had been lifted from her shoulders.

"Getting the alarm system has definitely taken away a lot of my stress. Now, are you ready to start our treasure hunt?"

"I'm more than ready," he replied.

"I thought we'd start out on the top floor and work our way down."

"Sounds like a logical plan to me," he agreed.

Minutes later they were in one of the large rooms on the third floor. The walls were papered with a gold-flocked paper. "I'm not even sure what I'm looking for," she said.

"We just need to run our hands over the walls and woodwork and see if we feel any irregularities."

He started on one side of the door and she started

on the other side. "Tell me about your ex-wife," she said, the question surprising him. "I feel like I told you a lot about Blake, but you really haven't told me much about the woman you married. Where did you meet her?"

"I met her my sophomore year in college. We were both business majors. We dated for two years and then got married six weeks after we graduated." He continued to run his fingers across the wallpaper as he talked.

"What was she like?"

"She was an attractive blonde, bright and driven to have a perfect life."

Eliza released a small laugh. "I wouldn't even know what a perfect life looked like."

"Sherry knew. She had a picture in her head of perfect and that's the way she wanted things. She picked out the house and all the furniture. She told me exactly how she wanted the landscaping done. She decided we'd only have one child because she didn't want motherhood to interfere with her work. Now that I look back on our marriage, she was actually quite controlling, but at the time I didn't mind. I just wanted to make her happy. She'd had a pretty rough childhood. Both her parents were messy alcoholics, so I understood Sherry's need for control and order."

"Were you happy?"

Troy hesitated for a long moment before answering. "Sherry and I had our ups and downs, but for the most part I was happy. I was really happy the day that Annie was born." His heart hitched at the memory of that special day. It had been the absolute best moment of his life. "I'd always wanted to be a father."

Eliza turned and looked at him, her gaze soft. "Tell me about Annie." She sat on the floor and crossed her legs and gestured for him to do the same. "Tell me all the wonderful things about her."

He sat down facing her as a rush of memories overtook him. "Sherry and I used to tell people that Annie didn't learn to walk. Instead she learned to skip and jump and run. She was exuberant and so curious about everything in life."

Eliza reached out and took one of his hands in hers. "Was she a princess or a warrior?"

"Definitely a warrior, although Sherry tried her best to make Annie a princess. There wasn't a dress in Annie's closet that wasn't torn or grass-stained. Ruffles were ripped and hair ribbons got lost."

He smiled as memories continued to cascade through his mind. They were the memories he hadn't accessed since the horrible day that had changed his life forever.

"Tell me more," Eliza encouraged him.

And he did. For the next thirty minutes he told her

about all the special, funny and loving moments in Annie's life. He told her about a pet frog that she'd found in the backyard when she was five and how she loved to sing songs he and Sherry played on the radio when they were in the car.

He talked about how the little girl hated bullies and loved the underdogs. He told Eliza everything he could think of to paint a picture of how wonderful, how very special, his daughter had been.

When he was finished he was filled with a strange happiness and a sense of release. He suddenly realized that since her death, he'd forgotten to remember her life.

He squeezed Eliza's hand. "Thank you."

"For what?" she asked curiously.

"For helping me remember all the love and happiness Annie brought into my life." He released her hand and stood. "And now let's get back to work. We've got a mystery to solve."

They only managed to clear the one room before it was time for Eliza to head to the bus stop. "I'll take the walk with you," he said, knowing that any more searching would have to wait until the next day when the kids were once again in school.

"Mr. Troy!" The children each greeted him with excitement as they got off their school buses. They were obviously thrilled that he was at the bus stop with their mother. They talked over each other in an effort to tell him all about their day.

By the time they reached Eliza's house he'd learned that Mary, a stuck-up classmate of Katie's, had thrown up in class that day and nobody had felt sorry for her. Sammy told Troy that he was learning braille and that his teacher had brought in a bunny that day for all the class to pet.

"Are you coming in to have snacks with us?" Katie asked when they reached Eliza's front door. "Maybe if you have snacks with us then Mommy will let us have cookies again today."

Troy laughed. "I'm sorry, honey, but not today," he replied. "I've got some paperwork I need to get done so I need to get back to my house."

Eliza frowned. "I'm taking up too much of your time."

"Nonsense, and I want you to stop saying that. I'll see you tomorrow afternoon."

"Will you meet us at the bus stop again?" Katie asked.

"We'll see," he replied. With last goodbyes said, he headed back to his home. A new lightness filled him as he went into his house and headed for the kitchen. He made himself a cup of coffee and then carried it to his desk in the corner of the living room.

Taking a sip of the hot brew, he leaned his head

back and closed his eyes. He felt as if something profound had occurred, and that "something" was he'd gotten back his memories of happiness and love with Annie.

For too long his brain had focused only on the pain and anger of her loss. For the last three years he'd remembered only her death and had thought nothing of her glorious but too-short life.

He knew those bad memories would be back, especially in less than two weeks when it was the official third anniversary of Annie's disappearance and death. But now he'd finally reclaimed the good memories to help him through, and he could thank Eliza for that.

He opened his eyes and got busy working on payroll. It usually took him several hours to complete and today was no different. He stopped once to make himself a ham-and-cheese sandwich and then got back to work.

It would have been easy for him to have an accounting company take care of payroll every two weeks, but as he checked hours and wrote checks for his many employees, he always felt a huge sense of pride. He'd started with nothing and had managed to build a small empire through hard work and hustle and some lucky breaks along the way.

Once the work was finished, he vegged out in

front of the television until just after ten. He then got up and retrieved his gun from his nightstand. He carried it and a cleaning kit to the kitchen table.

At some point during his veg time, he'd decided it would be a good idea not only to clean and oil the gun, but also to make sure it was fully loaded.

If there really was a multimillion-dollar necklace hidden someplace in Eliza's house, then he couldn't begin to guess to what ends the bad guy or guys would go to get it.

All of his stomach muscles tightened at the thought of any danger coming close to Eliza and her children. Certainly, the security system made him feel somewhat better, but they had no idea what might happen next.

The only thing he knew for sure was that somebody might believe a multimillion-dollar necklace was worth killing for, and that definitely had him worried.

Chapter Eight

She awakened with the scent of Blake in her nose, that particular scent that she knew so well. She sat up and shoved her hair away from her face, confused for a moment with the grogginess of lingering sleep.

Had she been dreaming about Blake? Had her mind played a trick on her and made her think she smelled her ex-husband's cologne? The last place Blake's ghost would be was here with her and the children. He hadn't really wanted to be with them when he was alive.

If he was haunting anyplace it would probably be a popular club or another woman's bed. Unless he'd gone to hell, and his own particular hell was being connected to Eliza and the children through eternity.

She almost laughed aloud at this thought. There was that wild imagination that Troy had talked about her possessing.

The room was lit with the faint rise of the sun. She

flopped back to her pillow and drew a deep breath. There was no question about it, the house was making her more than a little bit crazy.

In the past couple of days she and Troy had managed to clear the entire upper level. They had only found one secret compartment next to a heater vent. The compartment had held only musty air.

In that time she'd learned more about Troy and he had learned more about her. They had shared some deep conversations about their childhoods and what events had helped shaped them into adults. And they had shared silly talks, telling bad jokes to each other and chatting about the kind of nonsensical stuff that had deepened their connection.

And tonight she was going to Troy's for dinner. Her heart skipped a beat at thoughts of what the night might bring after the meal.

She wanted him. She wanted him not just as a helpful neighbor, but as a friend and lover. She wanted him not just for a night, but potentially for a lifetime.

As this week had passed and she'd seen him interact with her children, she'd realized she was very close to being in love with him completely. He not only made the kids laugh, but he also made them feel a sense of pride about schoolwork and chores completed. Even when Katie had gone into meltdown mode last night when they had all been sharing dinner, he'd shown tremendous patience and understanding to a little girl who had not wanted to eat her green beans.

She knew without question he would not only be a great husband, but also be a terrific and loving stepfather. And she wanted that for her children, who had never really known any love from their own father.

The truth of the matter was that she wasn't close to being in love with Troy, she was in love with him. But she still had no idea what his feelings were toward her. Oh, she knew he enjoyed her company and there was no question he entertained a healthy dose of lust for her, but where did he see them going in the future? What were his intentions for their relationship?

"Stop it, Eliza," she whispered to herself. Just because she knew where she was where Troy was concerned didn't mean he was at the same place. She was the first one to admit that things had happened quickly between them.

Her love for him had sprung to life hard and fast, surprising even herself. It very well might take him more time to get to where she was…and she was willing for him to take that time if it meant a life with him forever.

Or was it possible this house and the danger she

sensed around her was tricking her into believing she was in love with Troy because he felt like safety? She didn't want to believe that. The love she had for him felt completely separate from the mystery of the house. Her love felt real and true.

She could stay here in bed all day and worry about all the questions that flew around in her head, but reality was she had breakfast to make and children to wake and another workday ahead of her.

Minutes later she was dressed and in the kitchen making pancakes. "Can I have whipped cream on mine?" Katie asked.

"Me, too," Sammy added.

"How about whipped cream and strawberries," Eliza replied. At least she didn't have to worry about what was for dinner tonight. She'd be eating at Troy's and the kids would be dining wherever Lucy took them.

"I can't wait to slumber party with Ms. Lucy tonight," Katie said right before she shoveled a huge bite of pancake into her mouth.

"Me, too," Sammy agreed. "She lets us stay up real late."

"How late?" Eliza asked.

"Ten o'clock," Katie said. "And we always have something good for bedtime treats."

"That definitely sounds like a fun slumber party,"

Eliza replied. At least they didn't ask again about when they were going to have a slumber party with Mr. Troy. Tonight it was possible she'd have a slumber party with Mr. Troy, and it would be a party for two.

With breakfast eaten, she hurried them up the stairs to get dressed for school. She'd already seen to it that each of them had packed an overnight bag complete with toothbrushes and clean underwear.

An hour later the kids were gone and Eliza was at her desk working. She'd finished the big job of the web page for the doctors and today she was starting to build a page for a romance author. She was definitely looking forward to this particular job. She had lots of beautiful book covers and fun information from the author to help her build a vehicle that would give the author more visibility.

She stopped at noon to stretch and make a salad for lunch. When her brain wasn't focused on her work, it went to thoughts of Troy and the night to come.

They had agreed that she would walk over to his house around six. That would give her about two hours after the kids left to get ready and make a dessert.

You can be dessert. His words played and replayed

in her head, flushing her body with warmth. She quickly finished her salad and then got back to work.

It was just after two when her doorbell rang. Instantly every nerve in her body tensed. She wasn't expecting anyone. Lucy wouldn't be here until after school and Troy hadn't planned to be here at all today.

The last time her doorbell had rung it was a man impersonating a utility worker who wanted to get into her house. She got up from her desk and walked over to her window. She peered out in an effort to see who might be on her porch, but whoever it was was standing so close to the door it was impossible for Eliza to see.

Another knock sounded and Eliza left her office and went to the front door. Her heart thundered the frantic beat of fear. Her hand trembled as she reached out, and before she could grasp the doorknob she dropped her arm back to her side.

She was too afraid to open her own front door. How on earth had this happened? She had no idea how long she stood there with deep, shuddering breaths releasing from her in noisy gasps.

The knocks stopped and still she remained frozen in place. She finally turned off the alarm and managed to wrap her hand around the doorknob and pull it open. Hanging on the outside doorknob was a flyer announcing a new Chinese restaurant nearby.

Looking left and then right, seeing nobody around, she quickly opened the door and retrieved the flyer. She then slammed the door and relocked it, sickened by her own fear.

She turned the alarm back on and then sank down at the kitchen table and waited for her breathing to return to normal. Maybe she should just give up. Maybe she should leave the house to some charity and she and the children should go back to apartment living.

That way the secrets of the house would no longer endanger her or the kids. She'd no longer be afraid to open her own door. Without having to pay rent or a mortgage, she'd been looking forward to being able to slow down a bit with the work and enjoy more fun times with her kids. Leaving this house would require her to go back to the rat race of longer hours working and worrying about finances.

And of course, she'd be moving away from Troy. But what really bothered her was the idea of the kids once again being cooped up in an apartment.

She loved seeing Sammy sitting at the picnic table in the backyard, his face raised toward the sun. She'd watched as they played with miniature cars on roads they'd made in the dirt. The kids absolutely loved the yard and she didn't want them to go back to the way they had lived before…only going outside when she could take them to a local park to play.

She mentally shook herself as a touch of anger rose up inside her. What was she doing sitting here and thinking about giving up this house? It wasn't just a house, it had become the kids' home. Dammit, it had become her home and she wasn't going to be chased out of it by anyone or her own damn fear.

What she needed to do was find every hiding place there was in this house, and if there was a necklace in one of them, then it needed to be turned over to the proper authorities.

She absolutely, positively was not going to be chased out of this house by ghosts, or some aging jewel thief looking for a necklace that had probably been fenced years ago by a man who was now dead.

With this thought in mind she marched up the stairs and into Sammy's room. She couldn't sit around, wasting hours waiting for Troy to come over and help her. She needed to help herself.

When it was time to get the kids home from the bus stop, she'd managed to clear Sammy's room. She'd touched every inch of his walls and had found nothing.

She and the kids had only been home for about fifteen minutes when Lucy arrived. The short, slightly plump woman had skin the color of rich mahogany and a smile that could light up the deepest dark.

Eliza led her into the kitchen. "Do you want a cup of coffee before you take my kids and run?"

"No thanks. I'm saving up all my calories so I can join your children in a complete sugarfest before I bring them home to you tomorrow morning," Lucy replied with a laugh.

"Thanks," Eliza replied drily.

"Actually, I'm planning to drive through a fast-food place and then take our dinner to the park by my house. Katie loves to climb the jungle gym there and Sammy likes to swing."

"Sounds like a nice time," Eliza replied. She knew no matter what they chose to do, Lucy would take good care of the kids.

"Where are my munchkins?" she asked.

"Upstairs. They apparently didn't hear you come in. Are you ready for them now?" Lucy nodded and Eliza moved to the bottom of the stairs. "Hey kids… Ms. Lucy is here."

There followed a chorus of excited yells as they both came down the stairs with their overnight bags in hand. Lucy hugged them both and then straightened. "Are you two ready for your night of adventure?" she asked.

"Yes!" they both exclaimed. "Are we going to have ice cream tonight?" Sammy asked.

"I see great big build-your-own sundaes in your near future," Lucy replied. The kids once again erupted with happy cheers.

"With sprinkles?" Katie asked.

"With pink sprinkles," Lucy replied.

There was a flurry of hugs and kisses and then they were gone and Eliza was left with only thoughts of the night to come with Troy.

She had two hours to make a dessert and take a nice bubble bath. In two short hours she'd walk over to his house and their evening together would begin.

As she prepared her version of a simple strawberry shortcake to take with her, her mind was filled with one simple question.

Was she going to make love with Troy tonight?

IT WAS CRAZY that a simple dinner date with a beautiful woman could make Troy so nervous. At the moment he couldn't tell whether it was anxiety or excitement that had him pacing the floors at a few minutes before six.

The house was clean. Dinner was in the oven warming. He was showered and he'd changed the sheets on his bed...just in case. One thing was for certain, Eliza would be in complete control tonight.

If she didn't want to sleep with him then that was okay. They'd have a good dinner and enjoy their time together.

So why did he feel so anxious? In the back of his brain he knew the answer. The anniversary of Annie's death was approaching in a week, but it wasn't something he intended to think about tonight. Tonight was all about Eliza.

At precisely six o'clock his doorbell rang. He opened the door and nearly lost his breath at the sight of her. "You look stunning," he said as he took the plate she carried from her.

Her dove-gray sundress clung to every curve and perfectly matched her eyes. The round neckline was low enough to give him a tantalizing peek of the tops of her full breasts, and her hair hung in shiny dark waves around her shoulders.

"Thank you," she replied. "Something smells delicious."

"That would be dinner." He led her into the kitchen and gestured her to the table, which was already set for a dinner for two. "I hope you're hungry."

"I'm starving."

"Good, I've been slaving over a hot stove all day long and everything is ready to serve. Wine?"

"I'd love a glass."

He served her red wine and as he pulled a salad

out of the refrigerator and sliced up the garlic bread, she told him about Lucy White.

"It's nice for the kids to have her in their lives. She's like an indulgent grandmother or a favorite aunt." She finished as he took the tray of lasagna out of the oven.

She grinned at him. "You know, if you want a woman to believe you cooked all day for her, then you might want to take the food out of the restaurant take-out container to bake it."

He returned her grin. "Ah, busted. At least I did make the salad."

"And it's a fine salad," she replied.

"And Garozzi's makes awesome lasagna."

The meal was one of the most pleasant ones he could ever remember having. She raved about the lasagna and they talked about politics and argued about football teams. She was a hometown fan of the Kansas City Chiefs, and he liked the Oakland Raiders.

They spoke of places where they'd like to vacation and each agreed that Hawaii was at the top of the list. Without the children it was a time to talk a little more in depth about a variety of topics.

He learned that her favorite color was peach and her dream for Sammy was a Seeing Eye dog when he turned sixteen. He also learned that she'd never felt truly loved by her husband, which broke a piece of his heart for her.

When dinner was over they carried coffee into the living room and settled in on the sofa. "This has been so nice," she said. "I love my kids, but a little adult time without them is always healthy."

"Thank goodness for Lucy White."

She smiled. "Yes, thank goodness for Lucy."

"What do you normally do when she has the kids for a night?"

"I take a bath. I always take a sinfully long bath. That's one of the first things you give up when you become a mom."

He leaned toward her and reached out to stroke a strand of her hair. He'd been longing to touch her from the moment she had entered his home. "And I'll bet you use bubble bath."

"Definitely. I like lots and lots of bubbles." Her breath caught as his fingers stroked down her cheek in a languid fashion. "And candlelight."

The vision of her in a tub full of bubbles, her bare shoulders gleaming in the glow of a candle, exploded in his head. The only thing that would make the vision better was if he were there with her.

"Have I told you how stunning you look tonight?" His breath was a warm caress on her neck.

"Why, Mr. Anderson, are you trying to seduce me?"

"Definitely," he replied. "How am I doing?"

"Unbelievably well," she murmured.

He then covered her mouth with his. Kissing Eliza fed some part of his soul, a hungry part he didn't know he possessed until his lips touched hers.

She leaned into him and opened her mouth so he could deepen the kiss. And he did. His tongue swirled with hers in a dance that shot heat through every part of his body. His hands reached up to stroke the soft, silky strands of her hair.

He didn't just want this woman, he felt as if he needed her. She was the air that he breathed, the food that he ate. She was the life-sustaining water for his thirst.

It didn't take him long to know that he wasn't going to be satisfied just kissing her on his sofa. He pulled back from her and gazed into her eyes, pleased to recognize hungry desire in their gray depths.

"Eliza, you know I want you."

"And I want you, Troy." Her lips trembled slightly.

He got to his feet and held out a hand to her. "Will you go upstairs with me?"

In her hesitation, his heart nearly dropped to

his feet. Was she about to turn him down? Okay, he would just have to deal with that. If she wasn't ready, then he would respect that. He knew she was a woman who didn't take this lightly. But after the long pause, she stood and slipped her hand in his.

Neither of them spoke as he led her up the stairs and into his bedroom. His heart beat hard and fast in his chest as adrenaline pumped through his veins. He couldn't ever remember wanting a woman as much as he wanted Eliza at this moment.

When they stepped into his bedroom he pulled her into his arms, and as he kissed her once again she molded herself against the length of him.

Oh, sweet, sweet Eliza. The press of her breasts against his chest, the warmth of her body so close to his, heightened his desire for her to a fever-pitch level.

"I want you naked and in my bed," he groaned as he tore his lips from hers.

"I want to be naked and in your bed as long as you're there with me," she replied.

He reached around her to the zipper at the back of her dress. It whispered down and he pulled the dress from her shoulders. It fell straight to the floor and pooled at their feet and left her clad only in a lacy white bra and a pair of wispy white panties.

It took only seconds for him to undress and for

them to be beneath the sheets. Her soft skin warmed him as their legs entwined and their lips found each other again.

He was so impatient. It didn't take long before the barriers of her bra and panties and his boxers became irritating deterrents. He took the offending underclothing off her and then kicked off his boxers.

Then it was just the two of them gloriously naked beneath the clean white sheets. He loved her breasts with his tongue, licking each turgid nipple as she moaned her pleasure.

She tangled her hands in his hair and then slid them down his back, each touch further igniting the flames inside him. Her scent surrounded him, that wonderful smell that was specifically hers.

He slid a hand down her stomach, wanting to touch her and bring her so much pleasure that she cried out his name as she climaxed.

And then he was there…in the soft folds of her. She gasped and shivered and then opened her legs wider to allow him complete access.

He moved his fingers against her, slowly at first and then faster as he felt the tension rising in her body. She clutched at his shoulders as her entire body stiffened. She moaned his name as she shuddered and then her body relaxed.

"Take me now, Troy," she whispered urgently.

He complied. He first leaned over and reached into his top drawer to retrieve a condom. He quickly rolled it onto his hard length and then moved between her thighs and eased into her. For a moment he didn't move other than to close his eyes and revel in the sensations that nearly stole his breath away.

He opened his eyes and gazed down at her as he began to stroke inside her. Her eyes glowed a smoky gray and her hair was a dark cloud against the white pillowcase.

Just looking at her stirred him to another level and his thrusts grew faster and more frantic. She met him thrust for thrust as she clung to his shoulders.

"Oh yes…yes," she cried out. He knew she was reaching a second climax and when she did, he was there with her.

He collapsed to his elbows above her and waited until his breathing returned to normal. He then smiled at her. "That was the best dessert I've ever had."

She laughed. "Ah, but you haven't had my special strawberry shortcake yet."

"I can tell you already there's no way a strawberry shortcake, no matter how special, can compete with this." He moved a strand of her hair away from her face. "Spend the night with me? I want to sleep with you in my arms."

She hesitated only a moment and then nodded. "I'd like that."

"Good, now don't move and I'll be right back." He got out of the bed and hurried into the adjoining master bath. He cleaned up and then pulled on one of his bathrobes. He carried a second robe back into the bedroom. "Why don't you put this on and we'll go down and eat some of that special strawberry shortcake."

"Sounds like a plan," she agreed. She sat up and pulled the robe around her and then together they left the bedroom.

"I feel like a teenager sneaking downstairs to eat something my parents don't think I should have," she joked.

"That makes two of us," he said with a laugh.

She did the honor of serving them the dessert while he made two cups of coffee. "This is delicious," he said a moment later when they were both seated at the table and he'd taken a bite of the dessert. "It tastes better than just ordinary strawberry shortcake."

"Thank you. I have a secret ingredient."

"What is it?"

Her eyes lit with a teasing light. "Now, if I told you, it wouldn't be a secret anymore."

"What other secrets are you holding back from me?" he asked, and then took another bite.

"None," she replied easily. "I don't have any deep, dark secrets haunting my soul. What about you?"

The conversation that had begun so lightly took a definite dark turn as he thought of the secret that burdened his soul. "I've got a secret that makes me a bad man," he replied.

She put down her fork and gazed at him steadily, as if sensing the darkness that had suddenly slammed into him. "I can't imagine you doing or thinking anything that makes you a bad man."

He shoved his dessert aside, his appetite momentarily gone. "I hate a man so much I wish him dead."

She smiled at him. "Troy, that doesn't make you a bad man, that just makes you human. I completely understand your hatred and your wish for his death."

He looked at her in surprise. He'd expected some condemnation or at the very least a lecture on how bad it was to harbor hatred in his heart. Instead she understood it. That definitely surprised him and oddly made him feel even closer to her.

"Next Saturday will be the third anniversary of Annie's murder." He'd felt the weight of it pressing down on him throughout the past week. It was like a dark cloud approaching that would obscure all the lightness in the world.

Eliza covered one of his hands with hers. "What do you need from me to get through it?"

Once again he looked at her in surprise. "What do you mean?"

"I mean would you like maybe a picnic or something else I could plan to help you get through the day? Or, if you're planning on working all day then would you like to spend the evening at my house to keep your thoughts occupied?"

"I'm usually not good company on that day. I just prefer to spend it by myself."

"Okay, but if you change your mind you know where I am." She gave his hand a final squeeze and then released it.

It was at that moment Troy realized he was in love with Eliza...and he definitely didn't want to be.

Chapter Nine

Eliza lay across Troy's naked chest. They had just made love for a second time and each and every inch of her body was sated. He was an incredible lover, passionate and demanding yet tender and giving.

Blake had been a selfish lover, only taking his own pleasure with her and not thinking about hers. She'd believed at the time that it was just the way men were. But not Troy...thank goodness for Troy. She'd never been taken to the heights of passion so wonderfully.

For the last fifteen minutes or so they had been making small talk until they got drowsy enough to sleep. "There was a knock on my door today," she said. She told him about the person leaving a flyer on her door.

"I had that same flyer on my door when I got home from work this afternoon," he replied.

"Yes, but it made me so damned angry to be afraid

to open my own front door," she continued. "Nobody should feel that way in their own home."

He gently stroked her hair. "I'm glad you were cautious. The security system won't work if you let somebody into your home or if you open your door to a stranger."

"But it's not right to be that afraid in your own home," she repeated. "It made me so upset that for a moment I thought about just giving the house to a charity and moving into an apartment where there's nothing hidden in the walls."

"I hope you didn't seriously consider that. I'm not ready to give you up as a neighbor." He kissed the side of her face. "Right now you're my favorite neighbor."

She smiled. "I considered it for a full minute before I got mad and stomped up to Sammy's room and checked every inch of it."

"And I'm assuming you found nothing."

"Absolutely nothing," she replied with frustration. "But this isn't going to chase me out of my house. My biggest concern right now is if we check the entire house and we don't find anything, how do we let the bad guys know that there's no necklace or any other jewels there?"

He was silent for a long moment, obviously thinking. "I don't know. If we're sure there are no jewels in the house then maybe we need to contact a reporter and see if they'd be interested in doing some sort of a story about all of it."

"How would we know if the bad guys would see or read the story?"

"I have a feeling if we can get a news crew to come out to your house, the bad guys would know about it."

She frowned. "We keep talking about bad guys, but as far as I know it's only that Mitchell guy," she replied. "Do you think he's working with somebody else?" The idea of more than one person wanting to get into her house shot a quick chill through her.

He tightened his arms around her. "We can't be sure. Right now it appears that it's only Mitchell."

"Do you think he's watching the house?"

He leaned up and captured her lips in a quick kiss. "I think this subject is way too heavy for us to be having right before going to sleep."

"You're right," she agreed. All she really wanted to think about was how magically their bodies fit together, how splendid their lovemaking had been and how deeply she had fallen in love with him.

She closed her eyes as he continued to caress her hair in soft, languid strokes. She was excited to find out what happened next between her and Troy. She was certain they were headed to a lifetime of happiness together. As he continued to stroke her hair, she finally drifted off to sleep.

THE HOUSE BREATHED around her in large gasps and deep moans, becoming smaller and more oppressive with each exhalation.

She sat in the center of her bed, Katie under one arm and Sammy under the other. The room was almost dark, but not so dark she couldn't see big shadows moving around the room from place to place.

They were trapped on the bed, unable to get to safety as the dark shadows darted closer and closer and the room got smaller and smaller.

"Go away," she cried. Her heart pounded so fast and hard she feared it might explode. She had to stay strong for her children. She had to protect them from evil...and there was horrible evil in the room.

"There are no jewels here. Go away and leave us alone." But no matter how loud she yelled, the shadows continued to dart here and there and the walls of the house continued to move inward.

Suddenly Sammy was gone, sucked from her embrace into the darkness that surrounded them. Then Katie disappeared and Eliza knew the house had taken them from her and that's when a primal scream released from her.

"ELIZA!" THE DEEP male voice cut through the madness of the dream. "Honey, wake up." She came awake weeping with Troy pulling her into his arms.

"Honey, you're okay," he soothed. "Everything is okay. It was just a dream."

It hadn't just been a dream. It had been a terrible, horrible nightmare. As the visions she'd suffered in the dream flashed once again in her head, she shivered. Thank God it had just been a nightmare.

"I'm sorry," she said, quickly pulling herself together. "I'm so sorry I woke you."

"Don't be sorry. Do you want to talk about it?" His arms were a warm comfort around her.

Did she want to talk about it? "No, I'm fine now." She didn't want to talk about the nightmare. She didn't even want to think about it again. It had been far too horrifying.

They settled back with Eliza on her side and Troy spooned around her back. His arm was around her and even though she was comfortable and felt safe, it was a very long time before she finally fell asleep again.

She awakened the next morning with dawn light seeping in around the edges of the curtains. She was alone in the bed, although she thought she could feel a lingering warmth where Troy had slept.

She remained there for several long moments, thinking about the night they had shared. Other than her nightmare, the time spent with him had been magical. She'd forgotten what it was like to love and feel loved, to feel that tingle of excitement and sweet anticipation whenever she thought of a man.

It was delicious. She rolled over to his side of the bed and smelled his pillow where his scent was evident. She was glad she'd chosen to be with him.

What happened next between them? Had this been the beginning of something special and lasting, or had it been the end? She had to believe it was the beginning, that she and Troy had a future together. Oh, she wasn't looking for a proposal or even a statement of undying love from him. She just hoped they had lots of days and nights together in their future that would eventually lead to marriage.

The only blight right now on her future was the damned house and whatever secrets it might still possess. She shivered as she remembered the nightmare she'd had the night before. Hopefully within the next week or so she and Troy could finish clearing the rest of the rooms and then figure out what to do next to assure the safety of her and her children.

Eager to see Troy, she got out of bed, grabbed her clothes from the floor and then padded into the adjoining bathroom. Minutes later she headed down the stairs where the scent of fresh coffee and bacon beckoned her into the kitchen.

"Good morning." He greeted her with a smile and gestured for her to have a seat at the table. "How does bacon and an omelet sound?" He poured a cup of coffee and carried it to her at the table.

"Sounds wonderful, but what can I do to help?"

"Absolutely nothing. I've got this."

"I'm not used to having breakfast made for me," she said.

"It doesn't hurt for you to sit and let somebody else do the cooking. Besides, breakfast is about the only meal I can get right."

She sipped her coffee and watched him covetously. He was clad only in a pair of blue jeans. Nothing like bacon and a bare-chested hunk in the morning, she thought with a happy sigh.

"Did you get enough sleep despite my screaming bloody murder in the middle of the night?" she asked.

He flashed her a quick grin. "I slept great. You're a terrific snuggle bunny."

"Thank you, sir. I try." She released another happy sigh. She had wondered as she'd dressed if this morning would somehow be awkward between them. Instead it all felt wonderfully normal.

Breakfast was pleasant and all too quickly, he

was walking her home. "What are your plans for the day?" he asked as they reached her front porch.

"No real plans. I might do a little work but my focus on the weekends is usually doing fun things with the kids." She pulled her keys from her purse. "What about you?"

"I've got a couple of jobs to check out and that's about it."

"Do you want to come over for dinner tonight?"

He hesitated a moment and then shook his head. "Thanks, but I've got some things I need to take care of so I'll take a rain check."

"If you change your mind, dinner is always served around five."

"I'll keep that in mind. I'll see you later." He leaned forward and planted a lingering kiss on her forehead. "Now, get inside so I know you're safe and sound."

She unlocked her door and stepped inside to the control panel so no alarm would ring. With a wave to Troy, she rearmed the alarm and closed the door.

She still had an hour or two before Lucy brought the children home, so she headed upstairs for a shower and a change of clothes.

As she stood beneath the hot spray of water, her thoughts went over all the events of the night. She had already believed she was falling in love with

Troy. After last night there was no question in her mind. She was hopelessly, helplessly in love with him.

For the next hour she did some household chores, singing below her breath as she stripped the kids' beds and put on clean sheets. She started a load of laundry and then dusted the living room.

It was just after ten when Lucy and the kids returned home. "We have a new movie to watch," Katie said.

"Ms. Lucy bought it for us. It's about a dog and a cat who are best friends," Sammy said. "And it's for blind people. Can we watch it now?"

"First things first—what do you two say to Ms. Lucy?"

Both said their thank-yous and gave her hugs. "Can you stay for coffee?" Eliza asked her.

"I'd love a cup," she replied.

"Just let me get them set up in the living room and I'll be right back," Eliza said.

Minutes later the two women sat across from each other at the table. "I hope they were good for you," Eliza said.

Lucy smiled. "They are always good for me. They're terrific kids, Eliza, and you should pat yourself on the back for being a wonderful mother."

"Thanks. I am proud of them," Eliza replied.

"There's something different about you," Lucy said, her dark brown eyes gazing at Eliza with a sharp intelligence. "There's a sparkle in your eyes that I've never seen there before."

Eliza raised her hands to her cheeks and laughed. "Does it really show?"

"It's a man, isn't it?" Lucy released a burst of her own robust laughter. "Girl, you'd better tell me all."

"It's my next-door neighbor. His name is Troy Anderson and I'm pretty sure I'm in love with him." Saying the words out loud filled Eliza with an overwhelming feeling of happiness.

Lucy frowned. "And how does this Troy Anderson feel about you?"

Eliza thought about every minute she had spent with Troy. "I think he's falling in love with me, too. I know he cares deeply about me and we've been spending a lot of time together."

"This has all happened pretty fast, hasn't it?" Lucy's dark eyes held Eliza's in a steady gaze. "You only moved in here a little over a month ago."

"It has happened fast," Eliza admitted. "But in the last two weeks or so we've spent more time together than most people who have dated for months."

"And what do Katie and Sammy think about this new man in your life?"

"They absolutely adore him. He's really good with

them. If he weren't, then we wouldn't be sitting here and talking about him." She frowned at Lucy. "Why don't you look happy for me?"

Lucy reached out and grabbed her hand. "Oh, honey, you know I'm happy for you, it's just that I don't want to see you hurt."

"Hopefully I won't get hurt. Troy is like a dream come true and we get along wonderfully well. I'm looking for a happily-ever-after here."

"And I don't know anyone who deserves a happily-ever-after more than you." Lucy squeezed her hand and then released it.

"Why are you all alone?"

"I had my love of a lifetime years ago. We were magic together." A whisper of a smile curved her lips. It was there only a moment and then fell away. "Charlie and I had ten glorious years together and then he got cancer and he eventually passed away. After him I never wanted another man."

"Lucy, I'm so sorry."

"Don't be. I have the memories of ten beautiful years of loving and being loved to keep me warm on cold, lonely nights. I never wanted to be with anyone else. I'm happy with my memories."

"And you never wanted children?" Eliza asked.

"We wanted them and we tried to get pregnant,

but it just wasn't in the cards for us. That's one reason why I love your kids so much."

For the rest of her visit they talked about things happening at Sammy's school, the record-breaking heat and how much they were both looking forward to autumn.

"I'd better get out of here," Lucy said, and drained the last of the coffee in her cup. "I've got some errands to run and then laundry to do."

She stood and Eliza did the same and together they walked to the front door. "Thanks for last night," Eliza said.

"Don't thank me, you know I love having the kids over," Lucy replied. "I'll talk to you later and in the meantime, take it slow, Eliza."

Eliza gave her a hug and then Lucy was gone. Eliza returned to the kitchen and sat back down at the table. Lucy was right; things had happened fast between Troy and her. It was probably a good idea to take things slowly, but it was too late for that now. She was all in with Troy.

Already she couldn't wait to see Troy again. She wondered when she could be in his arms once again...when they might make love again.

She felt as if she'd waited a lifetime for a man like Troy to enter her life. Blake had been a nightmare, but she wouldn't wish her time with him away because he'd given her two beautiful children whom she loved to distraction.

Troy was a dream come true. Last night she had given him not only her body and trust, but also her heart and soul. Surely fate wouldn't be so cruel as to bring him into her life and then have him not love her back.

MONDAY AFTERNOON TROY sat in his truck at one of his job sites, his thoughts consumed with Eliza. He could leave right now and go to her house to help her clear another room or two while the children were in school.

Friday night had been a huge mistake. Holding her in his arms, making love with her and then sleeping next to her through the night had been a huge error in his judgment.

Because he'd loved it. Because he loved her.

He didn't want to be in love with anyone. He didn't want to love Eliza and care about her children, and he'd been a damned fool to let it happen.

Worse than his own feelings, he knew Eliza was falling in love with him. He'd tasted it on her lips, felt it in each and every one of her caresses. He knew it by the sparkle in her beautiful eyes whenever they were together.

He hadn't meant for this to happen. She'd entered

his life with such warmth. She'd not only made him find his laughter once again, but she'd also brought him such comfort when it came to the loss he'd suffered.

Things had happened so fast between them. Somehow she'd managed to knock down all the defenses he'd erected around himself for the past three years. She'd gotten into his heart so quickly he hadn't even realized it until this moment.

Now he had to make sure she understood that there was no future for them as a couple. He just wasn't willing to do it again. He didn't deserve to have it all again.

But he also didn't want to walk away from her with the jewel issue not resolved. With a deep sigh he started his truck and headed toward home. He'd take a quick shower and then go to Eliza's and help her with the search.

He was going to have to walk a fine line, being helpful and yet slowly distancing himself from her and the two kids. Still, it was difficult to remember his plan an hour later when she opened the door and greeted him with her gorgeous smile.

"I was starting to wonder if I was going to see you today," she said as she ushered him inside.

"I got held up on a job."

She frowned. "You know I never want to take you away from your work."

"I know, but I also know we need to finish checking out the house as soon as possible so you and the kids will truly be safe."

She grabbed his hand and squeezed it tightly. "And I'll never be able to thank you enough for your help and support through this." She released his hand. "I thought maybe we could get through Katie's room today."

"Sounds good to me," he agreed. Together they went up the stairs and to the little girl's room. There was more furniture and items in this room than there were in Sammy's bedroom.

"Here's the secret stairway Sammy found that leads down to the kitchen pantry," she said. To his surprise she opened a piece of the wall that revealed the narrow stairway.

"Interesting," he said. Who had once used that stairway and why had it been built into the house in the first place? Had Frank used it to escape arrest when he'd been a gangster? "Why don't we start by moving the bed out and checking behind it," he suggested.

For the next hour they checked all the walls in Katie's room. Thankfully the conversation remained light and there was no mention of the night they had spent together. He didn't want to talk about it. He didn't want to think about it—or the fact that sooner or later he was going to break her heart.

They found two hidey-holes in the walls. Both were empty. By that time the kids were coming home from school. He walked with her only to his house and then stopped. "I'll try to get over tomorrow, but I've got several big jobs going on right now and can't promise anything."

"You know what I said about your work." Her gaze held his for a long moment. "And I know this is probably a difficult week for you so whatever time you want to give me, I'll take. But I also understand if you need time alone."

God, why did she have to look so damned beautiful with the afternoon sun shining in her hair? Why did she have to be so damned understanding?

"Then I'll see you later," he finally said.

He intentionally didn't walk with her to the bus stop. He not only had to begin distancing him from Eliza but he needed to distance himself from her children as well. Still, the very thought made his heart hurt.

He should have never gotten so involved with Katie and Sammy knowing he had no plans to be in their lives long term. He knew they adored him, but they deserved so much better than him.

Minutes later he sat in his recliner and stared blankly at the television. He was trying hard not to think about the anniversary approaching on Saturday, but being in Katie's room had evoked memories of Annie.

She, too, had loved pink and her bedroom had been filled with pink ruffles and lace. She'd liked to climb trees and play rough-and-tumble, but she also liked a fancy little tea party now and then. She, too, had loved her dolls, especially one he had given to her when she'd turned three. That particular doll had been buried with her.

He shoved away these thoughts, knowing he would be immersed in and tormented by memories when Saturday came. He would wallow in those memories all that day and then he'd push them away for another time.

He went to bed early that night and tried to keep his mind completely empty. He didn't want to think about his daughter and he didn't want to think about Eliza and her loving, beautiful children.

Thankfully he'd scored another big commercial job for landscaping that should occupy him for the next couple of weeks. It was a new office complex that not only needed sod, but the owners also wanted several ornamental trees and hundreds of rosebushes and flowers planted. He was meeting a team of his men in the morning at the site to begin the work of laying sod.

For the next two days Troy worked until late and then wound up each evening at Garozzi's for dinner. Throughout each day it was thoughts of Eliza that intruded.

He missed seeing her. He wondered how her days had been and if she'd suffered any more nightmares. How well was Sammy getting along? Did Katie still have a crush on a little boy in her class named James or did she already have a new boyfriend?

He didn't like that he missed them all. He'd definitely allowed his emotions to spiral out of control where they were all concerned.

He was reminded of how much he'd always wanted a family of his own. His own parents had divorced when he was eight and he'd always sworn that when he got married it would be forever. He'd wanted a forever woman and children he would love and guide into adulthood. Eliza and her kids had renewed that longing inside him, but it was a longing he refused to fulfill.

Been there and done that, and fate had decided he couldn't have it and had ripped it all away from him in a single moment of looking away.

Thursday night he'd just stepped out of his truck when Eliza came out her front door with a plate in her hand. She hurried toward him, her smile warming him despite his wish to the contrary.

He couldn't help the way his heart lifted at the sight of her or the smile that curved his lips. "What have you got there?"

"Cupcakes for a hardworking man," she replied. As she got closer he saw six cupcakes on the plate. "I hope you like chocolate chip cupcakes with chocolate frosting."

"Sounds good to me. Thanks." He took the plate from her. "How have things been at your place?"

"Good. I managed to clear the guest room and the bathroom. I didn't find anything in either room. No hidey-holes and no precious gems."

"I'm sorry I haven't been able to help you out, but this new job has me working from dawn to dusk," he said.

She smiled at him. "Don't apologize. You told me you'd landed a new big project. How is it going?"

"It's going, but there's still a lot to do in a short amount of time. Is Katie still in love with James?"

She laughed, the sound wrapping around his heart like a ribbon filled with warmth. "No, apparently she saw James pick his nose and that grossed her out so badly she has now decided that she hates all boys except her brother and you."

"At least I'm in good company," he replied even

as his heart cringed. How could he make those two kids stop loving him?

Her gaze softened. "I've missed seeing you. How are you doing?"

"I'm doing okay. I've just been really busy, but I should get away for a little while tomorrow. We only have to get through your bedroom and then the second level will be done."

"If you can't get away, don't worry about it. I can clear my bedroom. I do wish you'd come by for dinner. The kids miss seeing you. I miss seeing you."

"I'll see what I can do," he replied noncommittally.

She looked back toward her house. "I've got to get back inside. I hope you enjoy the cupcakes." She gave him another one of her bright smiles. "Hopefully we'll see you tomorrow."

He watched as she headed back to her house and cursed himself for not putting an end to things with her. He should have told her that he intended to be a good neighbor and friend, but that's all he would ever be. He would never be a permanent part of her life in a romantic way.

He should have told her not to expect him for dinner ever again, but he hadn't. Dammit, he should have told her to stop smiling at him like he'd hung the moon. He carried the cupcakes into the house and set them on the island in the kitchen.

He then went back outside to get his mail and grab the morning paper that he hadn't had a chance to read that morning. He made himself a cup of coffee and then sat at the table with a cupcake and the mail.

How did you break up with a woman without breaking her heart? Could he get on the internet and find the answer? If he talked to Mike, would he have some advice on how to make everything better?

It couldn't be done. There was no way to break it off with her without breaking her heart. Maybe the best thing he could do was to be a total ass and piss her off so that she was the one who broke things off with him.

He sighed and took a bite of the cupcake. It was delicious, just as he'd expected it to be. Everything about Eliza Burke was delicious.

He finished the cupcake and then tackled the mail. An electric bill, a gas bill, three flyers that were gar-bage and then a plain white envelope addressed to him in block letters. There was no return address and no stamp.

Staring at the envelope, he tried to figure out who might have put a piece of mail in his box without sending it through the post office.

A sense of dread swept through him that he

tried to tamp down. Maybe it was some sort of a party invitation from a neighbor. Very doubtful. He didn't know any of his neighbors other than Eliza well enough to be invited to any party they might be hosting.

Advertising that had been hand-delivered, kind of like the flyer he'd found on his door the other day? No way.

He wouldn't know what it was until he opened it. He slid his finger beneath the seal, surprised to feel a photo tucked inside a folded piece of paper. He read the paper before looking at the photo.

HAPPY ANNIVERSARY. I MADE SURE YOU GOT A GREAT PRESENT.

He frowned at the bold block letters and then picked up the photo. He gasped in stunned surprise and immediately threw the photo to the center of the table.

He closed his eyes and drew in several long, deep breaths to get over the horrifying shock that rippled through him. He opened his eyes, steeled himself and then reached for the picture once again.

Dwight Weatherby was in a bed and obviously dead. His throat gaped open from a mortal wound and a *V* had been carved into his forehead. The blood was a vivid splash of red against the man's skin.

He was dead. The man who had kidnapped and raped Troy's daughter had been killed by one of the men with whom Troy had made the murder pact.

Which one of the men had killed him? Who in the group had taken the photo and then put it in his mailbox? The picture with the note felt gleeful and…sick. It was as if the killer was gloating and that bothered Troy.

Their pact had never been about torturing the men they wanted dead. It had always been about justice. But this murder didn't feel like justice; it felt like somebody enjoyed it.

Still, any normal human being would feel at least a little bit sorry for the horrific way the man had met his death. Troy had hated Dwight Weatherby more than anyone else on the face of the earth, but he'd always envisioned him dying by a single gunshot to the head or the heart. These were supposed to be clean kills, and there had been nothing clean about Dwight's death.

Still, he was glad the man was dead and that was why he couldn't…he wouldn't be with Eliza and her children. Because ultimately he was responsible not only for his daughter's death, but also for Weatherby's murder.

Chapter Ten

Eliza read about Dwight Weatherby's murder in the Friday morning paper. Instantly her thoughts were for Troy. What was he feeling? With the anniversary of Annie's death tomorrow he had to be relieved that Dwight Weatherby would never prey on a little girl again. Even she was glad that kind of man no longer walked the earth.

She'd been a bit disappointed all week by Troy's absence. She certainly didn't expect him to come over during his workday. But she had thought they might spend the evenings together, especially after the night they'd shared.

She'd thought about that night a lot during the past week and each time she did a rush of sweet warmth overtook her.

For the first time in years she wasn't afraid of the future. Owning the house without a mortgage had assured her a certain amount of financial stability, and having Troy in her life had filled an empty place she hadn't believed would ever be filled.

She was excited about the future, especially the one she envisioned with Troy. He was everything she could have ever dreamed of for herself and her children.

It was just after noon when the man of her dreams knocked on her door. "Hi," she said, and gave him a quick hug. He either hadn't worked that morning or had worked and then showered before coming over.

He smelled of sunshine and minty soap and the cologne that somehow always made her feel safe and secure. "I wasn't sure if I was going to see you today or not," she said.

"We need to talk." His gaze didn't quite reach hers.

"Okay. Why don't we go into the living room?" She thought she knew why he was so sober and… oddly distant. She'd seen the information about Dwight Weatherby's murder in the morning newspaper and he'd probably seen it, too. And the anniversary of his daughter's murder had to be playing with his head.

Moments later the two of them were seated on the sofa. "I saw it in the morning newspaper," she said. "You must be relieved…and satisfied."

One eyebrow quirked upward as he gazed at her

in surprise. "You think I should be satisfied that a man was brutally murdered?"

"That particular man, yes," she replied. Troy's features were drawn, as if he hadn't slept the night before. "You have to be glad that he's dead and will never be able to hurt a little girl again. The earth is far better off without him."

"I am happy, and I'm glad he probably suffered." The words seeped out of him on a whisper, as if he was ashamed of his feelings.

"Troy, don't feel guilty for that. It's perfectly understandable that you would feel that way about him. He did a horrific thing that destroyed your life and left you forever bereft. Besides, it's not like you're the one who murdered him. Somebody else couldn't stand the idea of that man being alive."

He frowned and stared down at the floor. "I've wished him dead over and over again for the last three years." He released a deep sigh and dragged his hand through his unruly hair. "But that isn't why I'm here or what I wanted to talk to you about." His voice held a touch of frustration.

"Then what did you want to talk about?" She wanted to reach out and touch him somehow. But his stiff posture didn't invite any kind of a touch. What was going on? A flutter of anxiety shot through her.

"I need to make sure we're both on the same page."

"And what page is that?" she asked slowly as the touch of anxiety swelled even bigger inside her. He looked so serious and once again his gaze didn't quite meet hers, but rather lifted to stare at a place just over her shoulder.

"The one where we're just having fun spending time together and you don't expect anything else from me." His gaze finally found hers and in the depths of his beautiful eyes she saw a distance she'd never seen there before.

Her heart dropped to the floor as all kinds of emotions began to bubble inside her. "I... I don't understand. I thought we were moving toward something really special."

Was he trying to break things off between them? Was this because of some crazy negative emotion that had him in its grip because of the murder of Dwight Weatherby or the anniversary of Annie's death?

Maybe if she told him how she felt about him it would stop whatever negative voices must be talking in his head. "Troy, I'm in love with you."

The words hung in the air for what felt like an agonizing eternity. He finally released another deep sigh. "Well, that's unfortunate."

His response to her heartfelt confession was like a slap in the face. His callous words momentarily stole her breath away. Unfortunate? That was his response to her baring her heart and telling him she was in love with him, that it was unfortunate? Confusion battled with hurt inside her and the pressure in her chest grew greater.

"Troy, why are you doing this? Why are you saying these things?" She wanted to shake him until the distance in his eyes cleared. She needed him to really look at her while he explained what was going on in his head.

"Because they need to be said. Eliza, I don't intend to get married again. Hell, I don't even want a long-term relationship in my life. I've enjoyed our time together, but I wanted to make sure you were clear about what to expect from me."

He looked so cold, with his features pulled taut and his eyes holding a hard glaze she'd never seen there before. Tears burned at her eyes as a sense of devastation filled her.

"You might have told me that before you took me to bed," she finally said.

"As I recall, you practically jumped into my bed without much prompting from me."

She gasped as his words stabbed through her like a knife. A rich anger filled her. "Don't you dare try to make me out as some kind of a whore. I slept with you because I'd fallen in love with you and I believed you felt that way about me, too."

Her voice trembled with her hurt. "Don't you dare try to cheapen me like that." She stared at him for several long moments, hoping he'd tell her this was all some kind of a bad joke and he hadn't meant any of it. But he remained silent and stoic.

"You've told me what page you're on, so I think we're done here." Once again hot tears pressed at her eyes as she stood.

She felt utterly blindsided and completely heartbroken. All she wanted now was for him to leave before her tears began to fall. She refused to allow him to see her cry.

He got up from the sofa and once again he didn't look at her as they walked toward the front door. When they reached the door he turned and gazed at her. He raised a hand, as if to touch her, but then dropped his arm back to his side.

"I'm sorry if I hurt you, Eliza. That was never my intention." His gaze turned soft and for just a moment she could swear she saw love there. It was there in his beautiful blue eyes only for a heartbeat and then gone as his eyes became shuttered and unfathomable again.

"I should have never let things get to the place they did without letting you know that I had no intention of having a deep and meaningful relationship. The very last thing I wanted was for you to fall in love with me."

She opened the door and remained silent. She didn't have any words left to respond to him. She was in a state of shock.

"I guess I'll see you around," he continued. "And you know if anything happens I'm right next door."

She gave him a curt nod and he walked out the door. She closed it after him, set the alarm and then leaned with her forehead against the wood.

In a single five-minute conversation, he had dashed all her hopes and dreams for the future. For several long moments she was too weak to move. The tears she'd fought against now released with explosive sobs.

How could she have been so wrong about him? About everything? There had been no red flags, no little alarm bells, absolutely nothing to warn her that this was coming. She should have known he was too good to be true.

She finally made her way back to the sofa where she collapsed in a heap. What had just happened? Why had it happened? She'd been so sure he was falling in love with her, that they were on the same page, but she'd believed it was her page where they continued to build to a marriage and her happily-ever-after.

How could she have been so wrong about things, so wrong about him? What had she missed? What had she overlooked to get it so darned wrong? These questions kept pounding in her brain as tears continued to fall.

She thought about each and every minute they'd spent together. She'd swear there had been no clues to warn her that he wasn't as into her as she was into him. Had she been just a one-night stand for him? She simply didn't believe that.

Did this have something to do with the death of Dwight Weatherby? Troy had obviously felt a bit guilty that he was happy the man was dead. Had his misplaced guilt played into what had just happened between them?

Or had he already entered a dark place in his mind due to the anniversary of his daughter's murder? A dark place where he didn't want and didn't believe he deserved any kind of happiness in his life?

A small nugget of hope made its way through the tears. Perhaps after tomorrow passed he'd realize just how important Eliza and her children were to him.

She quickly shook her head and shoved the hope away. She'd played that game before. It had been hope that had kept her in her bad marriage for as long as she'd stayed with Blake.

She'd hoped every day that Blake would suddenly make her a priority in his life. She'd hoped every day that he would suddenly wake up one morning and realize how much he loved his children. And each and every day she'd been bitterly disappointed.

She wasn't going to hope anymore. She had to move forward with the notion that she would be alone. She had to come to terms with the fact that Troy had been nothing more than a wonderful dream. But now she was awake, the dream was over, and she needed to face the cold, harshness of reality.

She'd be okay alone. She had been alone for most of her adult life. Even when she'd been married to Blake she'd been alone. She was strong and she didn't need Troy or any other man to make her whole.

Still, her heart ached as she thought of Sammy and Katie. They both adored Troy and they would miss having him in their lives. She hoped Troy remained kind to them and let them down easier than he'd just done her.

Her intention had been to clear her room today, but she didn't have the energy right now, not with her heartache so heavy in her chest.

She needed to take this time to cry all the tears she had inside, and then she would wash her face and put on fresh makeup so she could greet her children at the bus stop with a smile. Heartbreak didn't stop real life from happening.

In real life she still had a house that might hold more secrets. She had two children who deserved all her love and support, and somehow she had to figure out how to make Troy be nothing more to her than the neighbor next door.

IT HAD BEEN one of the most difficult things Troy had ever done. When Eliza had told him she was in love with him he'd wanted to take her in his arms and confess his own love for her.

But he hadn't. Instead he'd stolen any hope from her eyes, from her heart, and in the process had broken a piece of himself.

He'd been insensitive...cold and cruel, and it had broken his heart to be that way with her, to see the utter devastation wash over her beautiful features.

He'd stolen her smile, that beautiful, warm smile that he so loved to see. He wouldn't see that ever again. Oh, she might smile at him in passing, but it would be an empty gesture devoid of any warmth.

He now sat at his kitchen table and wrapped his cold hands around the heat of a cup of coffee. Despite the warmth of the house he was cold, and it was as if he would never get warm again. He kept seeing the pain in Eliza's beautiful eyes. The fact that he was responsible for that pain chilled him to the bone.

Eliza deserved better than him. He was damaged goods and was afraid to ever love again. He'd been careless with his daughter and it had resulted in her murder. He was also a man who had participated in a murder plot that had resulted in the brutal death of Dwight Weatherby.

He frowned as he thought of the horrific photo and note he'd received in his mailbox. Which of the other five men had killed Dwight? It really didn't matter now.

What bothered him was the gloating he'd sensed behind the note and photo, both of which he'd burned in his kitchen sink.

But burning the photo hadn't gotten the image of the dead man out of his mind. It was an unwanted vision burned into his brain forever.

Still, it was easier to focus on the photo than it was to remember the look on Eliza's face when he'd left her house. She'd looked…broken…defeated. As if he'd stolen all the life from her.

She'd be fine, he told himself. She was an amazingly strong woman and she'd get over this; she'd get over him. She was also amazingly beautiful both inside and out.

Eventually she'd meet a man who deserved to be

with her, a good man who would be eager to embrace both her and her children and they would all live happily ever after.

He wanted that for her, but the thought of her making sweet love with another man, the idea of her and the kids being happy with another man, also filled him with a wealth of sadness that he couldn't be that man for them.

He'd sworn to himself that he'd protect them all from any harm, especially when it came to the house and somebody wanting to get inside. But the security system she'd installed had brought him some peace with the issue. As long as she was smart as to who she opened the door to, she'd be just fine.

What he hadn't counted on, what he hadn't really expected, was him being the danger to her and the children.

And he couldn't sit here all afternoon feeling sorry for himself or Eliza. He swallowed the last of his coffee and then got up to put the cup in the sink.

He hadn't realized how long he'd been sitting and thinking until he walked outside to get into his truck and saw Eliza and her children coming down the sidewalk.

"Hi, Mr. Troy." Katie came running down the walkway toward him. Her eyes shone with happiness as she reached him. "I got an A on my spelling test today," she announced proudly.

"That's wonderful." He looked toward Eliza, who had slowed her and Sammy's pace. She didn't look at him but rather appeared fascinated by something across the street. It was a stab in his heart even though he knew this was the way it had to be from now on.

"When are we gonna have a slumber party with you again?" Katie asked, drawing his attention back to her. "Me and Sammy want to have one where we're awake and we can all play games and have fun and maybe eat ice cream with sprinkles."

"Oh honey, I don't think we're going to have any more slumber parties," he replied.

The sparkle in her eyes dimmed a bit. "But why? Don't you like us anymore?"

His heart constricted tight. What he wanted to do more than anything at this moment was to pull Katie into a big hug and tell her he loved her. But he didn't. Instead he smiled down at her. "Of course I still like you, but I'm too busy working to have slumber parties. In fact, I need to leave right now to go to work." He opened his truck door.

"Okay, Mr. Troy, see you later."

He waited until the three of them passed behind his truck and then he pulled out and headed in the opposite direction. The brief conversation with Katie had gutted him.

It wasn't just Eliza he'd fallen in love with, but also her bright, loving children. They deserved a far better father than he could ever be. After all, he'd lost his daughter because he hadn't been a good enough father.

What he needed now more than ever was work. He could go to the newest job site and plant flowers until dusk. And then he'd get up and do the same thing tomorrow. Maybe that was the best thing he could do on the anniversary—work until he dropped.

At least he could sleep at night knowing he had done one thing right. He had saved Eliza and her children from accepting less than what they deserved. And hopefully he could forget that he was walking away from love.

Saturday morning even before he got out of bed, the agony of this day three years ago slammed into him. Darkness descended all around him despite the early-morning sun creeping in through his light white curtains.

Maybe he should try to go back to sleep. At least if he did that he wouldn't have to think; he wouldn't have to feel anything. As he remained in bed he knew the sweet oblivion of sleep wasn't going to claim him again. He was wide-awake and already the pain of his memories was almost too much to bear.

Annie… Annie…his heart cried out.

Work. He'd go to the new job and work hard and hopefully that would keep his mind off anything else. With that plan in mind he pulled himself out of bed.

Forty-five minutes later he arrived at the job site where three other people were already at work. He greeted Bob Ryan, Skip Richards and Gary Hutchinson, three of his best workers.

"Where are Lynn and Jason?" he asked Bob, who was the working foreman for this particular job.

"Haven't seen or heard from them so far this morning," Bob replied, and cast Troy a wry grin. "You know those two, you can never depend on them on Saturday mornings. Too much partying on Friday nights."

"Yeah, well, they don't have to worry about coming in on Saturdays or any other days from now on," Troy replied tersely. He strode back to his truck.

He'd put off firing the two for a while now, but with pain and a simmering anger threatening to rage inside him, today felt like this was a great day to fire them. He called each of them and in both cases he got their voice mail. He left messages ending their jobs and then returned to Bob and the others.

"Monday I'll pull a couple of men from the hospital job to help you guys here," he said. "In the meantime let's get back to work."

As Skip and Gary began the task of laying sod, Troy joined Bob in planting flowers. It was really the wrong time of the year to be planting, but when Troy had approached the owner of the property about waiting until spring, the owner had been adamant that he wanted it all done now.

Within an hour Troy knew he needed to stop working. He wasn't in the right frame of mind to be around other people. He'd bitched at Bob twice about planting the flowers too close together and then had yelled at Skip for needing to take a break.

He apologized to all three men and then got in his truck and left the site. He drove around aimlessly and finally found himself parked at the curb in front of the house where he and his family had once lived.

He stared at the attractive four-bedroom brick house. He was shocked when instead of thinking of his time spent here with his wife, his thoughts filled with Eliza.

It was her smile he remembered, her scent that suddenly seemed to fill his head. Each and every moment he'd spent with her and her kids flashed in his head like a slide show.

Katie's impish grin; Sammy's shy, sweet smiles; their laughter at the pizza place and during other dinners shared. Eliza, wearing his robe after love-making. And the lovemaking that had been so amazingly good…

"No," the word whispered out of him. "No," he repeated more firmly. He didn't want to think of her or the children anymore. They were all now a part of his past. They had no place in his future.

He stared at the house once again. His time spent here with Sherry felt like another man's distant dream that had little to do with the man Troy was today.

But the memories of Annie in the house were raw and painful and suddenly flooding his brain. She'd taken her very first steps on the beige carpeting in the living room. She'd first said "da-da" when she was sitting on the kitchen floor banging pots and pans with chubby little hands.

She'd run to the front door with hugs and kisses to greet him when he got home from work, and he would carry her piggyback into the living room. It had been Eliza who had helped him have happy memories of his daughter, and he would always be grateful to her for that.

But this house also held the memories of horrified screams…of uncontrollable tears and angry words. It held the memories of a life ripped and gutted, of a family forever destroyed. He pulled away from the curb as a new darkness descended upon him.

He headed for home. A half an hour later he sat on his front porch. It wouldn't be long before the leaves would begin to turn colors with the winds and cooler temperatures of autumn.

The idea of the leaves dying only added to the darkness inside him. He released a deep sigh. He just wanted this day over.

He turned his head and was surprised to see Katie running across the lawn toward him. "Mr. Troy. Since you're not working now why don't you come over and play with us." Her eyes sparkled brightly. "Mom made cookies today and you could come over and eat some. They're peanut butter and they're really good."

"Katie, I'm not in the mood," he replied as kindly as he could.

"Maybe if I sit and talk to you for a little while, you'll get in the mood," she replied.

"I don't want to talk right now and you need to go home."

He must have said the words a bit harshly, for the sparkle in her eyes disappeared, her smile faded and her lower lip began to tremble. "You don't have to be so mean about it," she said, and then whirled around and ran for her house.

A deep remorse filled him, but then he told himself it was probably for the best. If the kids looked at him as the mean, grouchy neighbor next door then it would be easier for everyone.

He didn't know how long he'd been sitting on the porch when Katie appeared once again. This time she walked toward him with a sober little face.

He didn't speak to her, even as she sat down and then sidled closer to him. "Mommy told me today was a really, really bad day for you. She told me you had a daughter who is now in heaven like my daddy."

She slipped her little hand into his. "I just wanted you to know that I love you, Mr. Troy. I think God brought us together for a reason. You're a daddy without a daughter and I'm a daughter without a daddy."

His heart crashed against his ribs and tears burned hot at his eyes.

"Katie Marie," Eliza yelled from her front porch.

"Uh-oh." Katie released his hand and jumped to her feet. "I'm probably going to be grounded for a year. Bye, Mr. Troy...and remember what I said."

He would have watched her run back to her house, but he couldn't see for the tears that blurred his vision.

Chapter Eleven

"You are not to bother Mr. Troy by going into his yard without his permission," Eliza told her daughter when she flew through the front door. "You can say hi to him whenever you see him outside, but you are not to go into his yard. Now march yourself up to your room. You have an hour of alone time to think about how you broke the rules."

With a long face, Katie walked up the stairs. Eliza watched Katie, her heart aching for the children's loss of Troy.

She returned to the kitchen where Sammy sat at the table working on a wooden puzzle. "Does Mr. Troy not like us anymore?" he asked.

She should have never allowed Troy to get close to her children. Even if she and Troy had been dating, she should have kept Sammy and Katie separated from him.

She'd sworn at the time of her divorce that she

wouldn't bring a man into her children's lives until she was certain he was going to be a forever kind of man. She'd made a mistake with Troy. She'd told herself over and over again that things between them were moving too fast, yet she hadn't done anything to slow things down. She'd led with her heart instead of her brain. She would never, ever make that mistake again.

How did you tell a seven-year-old little girl that the man she loved didn't love her back? And how did she tell her sweet, blind boy that Mr. Troy would no longer have a place in their life?

"Mr. Troy cares about you and Katie, but he has his own life and lots of work to do," she finally said. Surely after a week or two of not having Troy here, the kids would be fine.

She had no idea how long it would take for her to feel fine. She wasn't anywhere close to being fine, but she kept a happy smile pasted onto her lips for her kids.

She still couldn't believe it was over. She still didn't believe he hadn't loved her. But she couldn't force him to be in her life no matter how much she loved him.

That night for dinner she made hot dogs and mac and cheese, two of the kids' favorites. Even though she knew better when she put the food on the table at five o'clock as usual, she wished for a knock on her door and for Troy to be there to join them.

As difficult as the day had been for her, she wondered how Troy had gotten through the agony of the anniversary of his daughter's death.

She couldn't imagine his pain. She couldn't imagine having the kind of horrific memories that must have filled his head all day long.

In a different world she would have been next to him, sharing that pain. She would have held him while he cried and done whatever she could to help him get through it.

Instead he had chosen to be all alone and there was nothing she could do about it except hurt for him.

After dinner she sat on the sofa and watched as the kids played cars in the secret hiding place that they referred to as their hideaway.

At least hearing the sounds of Sammy's and Katie's giggles helped her heartache. It had basically been just the three of them against the world for a long time.

Once again she assured herself that they would all be fine. The kids would continue to go to school and have time with Ms. Lucy and she would stay busy working on her website business and taking care of her children.

She had a full and happy life. Sure, Troy's presence in it would have been the cherry on top, but apparently it wasn't meant to be.

Bedtime was the usual ritual. Sammy showered first and then Katie took a bath. While Katie enjoyed her bubbles and bathtub paint, Eliza read Sammy a short story.

Within a half an hour the children were tucked in and Eliza went back downstairs to shut off her computer. She'd thought she might work a little bit after the kids were in bed, but she was too mentally and emotionally exhausted to do anything but go to bed herself.

She took a long, hot shower, got into her nightgown and then crawled into bed. It was only then, alone in the dark, quiet room, that tears that she'd held in all day began to fall.

She cried for what might have been, for what she thought would be. She wept for the kind and the wonderful man she'd fallen in love with, a man so damaged by life he would deny himself love.

Was it just her he didn't want to be with or did he intend to keep himself isolated and alone for the rest of his life? This thought broke her heart for him.

She fell asleep with tears still wet on her cheeks and dreamed of Troy and laughter and love. In her dreams he sat at the little purple-and-pink table in

Katie's room to share in a tea party, and then he sat on the sofa with an arm flung around Sammy's shoulders as they watched a movie.

And he was in bed with Eliza, his beautiful blue eyes glowing with not just desire and passion, but also filled with the forever kind of love she wanted from him.

In one minute she was in Troy's arms and in the next she was suddenly wide-awake, her heart beating a frantic rhythm. Immediately she reached for her nightstand lamp and turned it on.

She gasped as she saw her dead ex-husband stepping out of her closet.

Troy sat at his kitchen table. It was just after one in the morning and he'd been sitting here for hours nursing a scotch and soda and staring out at the moonlit landscape of his backyard.

He was trying hard to forget the feel of Katie's little hand in his. *You're a daddy without a daughter and I'm a daughter without a daddy.* All afternoon those words had played and replayed in his mind.

Along with thoughts of Annie.

Eliza had told him he needed to forgive himself even though she didn't feel like he'd done anything wrong. Could she possibly be right?

Three years ago he would have laid down his life

for Annie. He would have taken a bullet for her or been run down by a bus if it would have saved his daughter's life.

All you did was look away for a minute or two, a little voice whispered in his head. That had been his sin. He'd momentarily taken his eyes off his daughter. He couldn't have known that evil was near and just waiting to pounce.

Annie had known he loved her, because he'd told her so every single day of her life. A vision from the past suddenly filled his head.

He and Annie had been playing together and she began to tickle him. He wasn't really ticklish, but it was her giggles that made him laugh. She stopped tickling him and instead clapped her hands on either side of his face. "Oh, Daddy, I love your happy face," she'd exclaimed.

Instead of bringing him to tears, the vision brought with it a healing. In the past three years he'd been so focused on his own misery, he'd forgotten to remember that Annie had always wanted him to be happy.

Happy…like he had been with Eliza and her children. What was he doing killing himself slowly with isolation and guilt? Annie wouldn't have wanted that for him. She loved his happy face. At the moment his choices over the past three years felt like an utter disrespect to the daughter he had loved.

He tossed back the last of his drink and then rolled the glass between his hands. *You're a daddy without a daughter and I'm a daughter without a daddy.*

Was it possible fate was giving him a second chance at happiness? Annie would have wanted that for him. Hell, he wanted it for himself.

You've suffered enough, that inner voice whispered again. *You've virtually been dead for the past three years and now it's time to get back to living.* And living was Eliza and her children.

A sense of peace fluttered through him, a profound peace that held forgiveness for himself. He'd done enough penance. He'd punished himself long enough. And along with the peace came love.

He leaned back in his chair and allowed the rush of love that filled him. Yes, he wanted happiness in his life, and happiness was Eliza and Sammy and Katie.

If he could, he'd run across the yard to Eliza's place to tell her that he loved her, that he wanted a life with her. He'd tell her that he was ready to accept loving and being loved.

Of course he couldn't very well do that now. It was the middle of the night. An edge of anxiety filled him. Maybe she wouldn't be willing to give him a second chance.

He'd been pretty cold and hateful to her yesterday.

It was quite possible she wouldn't be able to forgive him. He'd pushed her away and there was a very real possibility that he'd pushed her away forever.

He shook his head. He couldn't think that way. He had to believe that somehow, someway she'd not only forgive him, but would also welcome him back into her life…this time forever.

What he needed to do right now was to get some sleep. He knew Eliza was an early riser and he wanted to be on her doorstep as early as possible in the morning, hopefully to reclaim her heart. He got up from the table and carried his glass to the sink. He raised his gaze to the window and froze.

Two figures were running to the back of his yard. They were clad in dark clothes, but the bright moonlight overhead made them visible. It was obvious by their body size that they were men.

They raced to the wooded area and then…disappeared. He frowned and squinted his eyes, seeking the two of them among the trees. But they were gone.

What in the hell was going on?

"BLAKE…YOU'RE…YOU'RE ALIVE," Eliza stuttered in stunned surprise. She stared in disbelief at the man she'd been married to and had thought was dead. She couldn't even begin to process that it looked like he had just walked out of her closet.

"Very much so."

"But…but I thought you died in a motorcycle accident."

"According to the world, I am dead. You know, good old Frank had a lot of thug friends. Many of them now live in Florida. It cost me a lot of money to fake my own death and get new identification, but I managed."

She continued to stare at him. He'd put on some weight since last time she'd seen him and his hair was longer. "But why would you do that?"

"One of the reasons was because I didn't want to pay child support for two kids I don't care anything about." His upper lip curled into an unpleasant smile. Oh, she remembered that smile, and she also remembered how very much she disliked him.

Still, her brain was spinning. What was going on here? How had he gotten into her closet? And why was he here? She raised the bedsheet closer around her. "How did you get in here?"

He released a small laugh. "I've been coming in and out of this house since you moved in here."

"But how? I've got a security system." And why hadn't an alarm gone off when he came into the house?

"A tunnel," he replied.

"A tunnel?" she echoed as her brain struggled to keep up with everything that was happening.

"Once again I can thank Frank. There's a tunnel that runs from your closet to the backyard next door. He made sure he always had an escape route if the cops came knocking."

He stepped farther inside the room and Mitchell also stepped out of the closet. The dark-haired man wasn't wearing an ill-fitting Kansas City Power and Light uniform tonight. Rather he wore dark jeans and a black T-shirt that stretched over his broad upper body. His dark eyes gleamed as his lips curved into a smile.

"Mitchell here got a little ahead of things trying to get in through the front door." Blake laughed once again. "We were quite amused when you put in that fancy security system because we knew it wasn't going to keep us out."

"So it was you I heard, the rustling and the bumps in the night."

"Yeah, it was hard to look around in here in the dark and sometimes we made a little noise."

Somewhere in the back of her mind she knew she was in trouble, but she was still struggling to fully comprehend Blake's presence here. "What do you want, Blake?" Thank God the children hadn't awakened to see their dead father.

"You know what I want: the necklace." He took a step closer to the foot of her bed.

She smelled the thick, acrid scent of danger in the room, the smell overriding Blake's familiar cologne. "What necklace? I don't know what you're talking about," she bluffed.

"Don't play stupid with me. You had to have found it. Mitchell and I have searched this entire place from top to bottom and all the hiding places are empty."

He took another step toward her, his eyes narrowed. "I know it was here because Frank told me it was here right before he died."

"When did you see Frank?" She was stalling, biding time, but she didn't know what she might be waiting for. The cavalry to ride in and save the day? That wasn't going to happen.

Blake and Mitchell had gotten into the house without setting off the alarms. Nobody knew they were inside and so nobody would be coming to help her.

"I managed to sneak into the hospital the day before he died," Blake said. "And he told me all about the robbery and the necklace. I know you have it, Eliza. I also know there's a big reward for the return of the necklace."

"You're probably planning on turning it in and getting that reward," Mitchell said. "I've got a one-half interest in those jewels from the heist and I've waited a long time, and tonight is collection time."

"Blake, I have no idea where any necklace is," she said desperately. "Please just leave."

"I can't just leave. You shouldn't have woken up, Eliza. Mitchell and me were just going to check out another couple of places while you were still asleep, but you made the mistake of waking up and turning on the light." Blake pulled a revolver from his waistband.

Eliza gasped, her heart beating so fast she could scarcely draw a breath. "Blake, what are you doing?"

"Whether you have the necklace or not doesn't really matter. We'll find it before dawn if we have to tear down all the walls in the house. But I can't let you live. I'm not going to let you ruin the new life I've built."

"I won't tell anyone I saw you. I swear I won't tell," she replied frantically. Oh God, what would happen to her children if she died? What would happen to her sweet children? The thought of them finding her dead body in the morning was too horrific to imagine.

"Blake…please don't do this." Tears burned at her eyes and slid down her cheeks. This couldn't be happening. Surely she wasn't going to be murdered in her own bed by a man who had once been her husband.

She looked around, as if help might magically appear out of thin air. The control panel next to the bed. If she could just get to it, she could make the alarm go off and hopefully help would come.

"Don't even think about it," Blake said. "If you even flinch, you're dead."

She looked at the gun in Blake's hand and realized he had a silencer on it. But she'd heard somewhere that even with a silencer gunshots were loud.

"Somebody will hear," she exclaimed. "Blake, if you shoot that gun in here somebody will hear it and come to see what's going on."

"I'm gambling that nobody will hear it," he replied. "It's the middle of the night and everyone is asleep and these walls are pretty well insulated." His eyes glittered with a sick light. "Let's give it a test." He raised the gun and Eliza said a quick prayer for her children.

Blake spun around and shot Mitchell in the chest. Eliza slapped her hands over her mouth to stanch her scream. Mitchell wore a bright red splash and a look of disbelief before he fell to the floor and within seconds appeared dead.

"I don't hear anyone coming," Blake said calmly. "And I really didn't want to share with him." He pointed the gun at her. "This is your last chance. Tell me where the damned necklace is."

"I don't know," she cried hysterically. "I swear I don't know."

"Mommy?" Katie's little voice made time stand still. *No. No. No!* Eliza's brain screamed.

Katie looked at Blake. "Daddy!" Her voice was filled with awe and delight as she ran to him and embraced him around his waist.

Eliza knew if something drastic didn't happen fast, it was possible that her blind son would be the only survivor of Blake's greed.

Chapter Twelve

The minute after Troy had seen the men in his backyard he'd grabbed his gun and a flashlight and headed out the back door. The night was hot, but a cold chill spiraled up his spine.

What had those men wanted and where in the hell had they gone? He ran across the backyard and didn't turn on the flashlight until he was in the area where the two men had seemed to vanish into thin air.

He'd never explored much back here, preferring to leave the area to the deer and other wildlife who called it home. Now he clicked on his flashlight and looked around. There were definitely no men hiding behind the trees or anywhere in the near vicinity.

Had they really been there? Or had they just been a figment of his imagination? No. No, he knew what he had seen. Somehow, someway those men had managed to disappear in this area.

He began to shine his light on the forest floor,

seeking something that might explain the sudden disappearance of the men.

He walked slowly from one tree to another. A rustling behind a bush whirled him around in time to see a rabbit running away. Insects whirred and clicked and buzzed around his head. But nothing distracted him from the task at hand.

There had to be something here. Why would two men run back here in the middle of the night? What had they been doing and, dammit, where had they gone?

He wasn't giving up until he had some answer that made sense. Once again he shone his light back and forth on the ground.

He froze as his foot hit something solid. He aimed the light down to see what appeared to be a corner of a piece of wood. He moved his foot from side to side, revealing a large piece of plywood.

What was it doing back here? Who had put it here? His heart quickened its pace as he revealed a small handle on the wood. A door? He grabbed the handle and pulled up, stunned when it rose up to reveal a tunnel going down into the bowels of the earth.

It explained how the men had disappeared, but where did the tunnel lead? He grabbed his flashlight more firmly in his hand and descended.

Six large steps down and then he was in the tunnel

itself. Earthen walls pressed in on him and he had to duck to proceed forward. And forward was definitely leading him in the direction of Eliza's house.

If this tunnel did, indeed, lead directly into Eliza's house, then a lot would be explained. But what terrified him at the moment was the fact that two men had entered this tunnel and might be in Eliza's house at this very minute.

This thought spurred him to move faster through the musty-smelling tunnel. All he could think about was that it was possible Eliza and the children were in danger.

He consoled himself with the thought that he suspected the men had used this tunnel before. The figure Eliza had seen in the dark had probably been somebody who had entered her home this way. So far they hadn't confronted Eliza, so hopefully she was still sound asleep and had no idea that the men were anywhere nearby.

It felt like he'd been walking forever when he came to a place where the tunnel divided into two. He stopped, unsure which direction to take.

Was it possible he'd somehow gotten disoriented and the tunnel didn't lead to Eliza's house after all? He shone his light first up one direction and then the other, cursing that his flashlight wasn't brighter, stronger. All he could see up both passageways was darkness ahead.

The unmistakable sound of a gunshot sounded and terror sizzled in his veins. Eliza! His heart cried her name as he stared at the two tunnels. Which one should he take?

He finally raced up the one that veered right, praying that he had made the right choice and he wasn't too late.

"DADDY, YOU AREN'T in heaven, you're here," Katie exclaimed happily. She looked at Mitchell's body and her happiness transformed to horror. "Is that man dead?"

"Get off me," Blake growled, and tried to pull Katie's arms from around him.

Eliza shot off the bed. "Don't you hurt her," she yelled.

Blake wrapped an arm around Katie with his gun still pointed at Eliza. "Then tell me where the necklace is."

"I can't tell you what I don't know," Eliza replied with fervor as tears tried to choke her. "Just let her go, Blake. You're scaring her."

"I got a new necklace," Katie said. "It was buried treasure I found in the wall."

Blake yanked the little girl around and grabbed

hold of one of her shoulders. "Where is it?" he screamed at the child. "Where is the necklace now?"

Katie began to cry…deep, wrenching sobs that made it impossible for her to respond. Eliza launched herself at Blake, momentarily blinded by her daughter's terrified distress.

Blake raised the gun and pistol-whipped her upside the head. She reeled backward and landed on the bed as pain exploded and stars flashed behind her eyes.

"Tell me, you little brat. Tell me where the damned necklace is," he screamed at Katie.

"Isabella wanted to wear it," Katie finally managed to sob.

"Who in the hell is Isabella?" Blake asked. "You better not have given it to another kid."

"She's…she's not a kid…she's one…one of my dollies," Katie managed to gasp out between her sobs.

"Go get her," Blake demanded. "Bring me Isabella." He released his hold on her.

"Mommy? What's happening?" Sammy appeared in the doorway.

Blood had begun running into Eliza's left eye from the blow she had taken, but that was nothing compared to the pain that ripped through her as she realized it was possible neither of her children would survive the night.

A still-sobbing Katie moved to stand in the doorway next to her brother. "Run, Katie," Eliza screamed. "Take your brother and run to your hideaway. Stay in there until I come and get you out."

She had no idea if Blake and Mitchell had found the hideaway in the living room or not, but more than anything she wanted her children out of this room where a dead man was on the floor and their father held a gun on her.

"Run, Katie," she cried. A hysterical sigh of relief swept through her as the two kids disappeared and their footsteps sounded down the hallway.

"It doesn't matter where they've gone," Blake said. "I imagine you know all of your daughter's dolls. You're going to go with me to her room and once I get the necklace I'm afraid I'm going to have to kill you. And then I'll find the kids and I'll kill them, too. Loose ends are never a good thing." He offered her a bloodless, evil grin.

Movement behind Blake in the closet drew her attention. Oh God, did he have somebody else coming to help him take care of the "loose ends"?

Blake laughed. "Don't think you're going to trick me by looking behind me. There's nobody coming to save you."

He'd just gotten the words out of his mouth when Troy exploded from the closet and slammed into Blake's back. Blake flew forward and his gun clattered to the floor.

Eliza screamed as Blake turned around and punched Troy in his jaw. The two men tumbled to the floor. Eliza scrambled off the bed and grabbed Blake's gun.

With a trembling hand she pointed it, but she couldn't fire it as the two men wrestled on the floor. She couldn't risk hitting Troy.

Troy finally managed to make it to his feet and pointed a gun at Blake. Blake stood and faced him, every muscle in his body bunched to spring.

"Go ahead," Troy said with deadly intent. "Give me a reason to pull the trigger."

Blake raised his hands. "I'll share with you," he said. "I'll give you half a million dollars to let me take the necklace and leave. I won't bother Eliza anymore and you'll never find me on this property again."

"Only half a million?" Troy replied.

Blake grimaced. "Okay, a million dollars. I'll give you a million."

Troy stared at Blake and said nothing.

"Think about it, man. A million dollars tax-free. Think about what you could do with that kind of cash," Blake said. "You can quit working and travel. Buy yourself a sports car or a new cool place to live. You can do anything you please with that kind of cash."

Troy shot a glance at Eliza, a deep frown cutting across his forehead. "Do you know this guy?"

"He's my ex-husband. He faked his own death so he wouldn't have to pay me child support."

"Did he do that to you?"

Eliza reached up and swiped at the blood on her forehead. She nodded at Troy. "He was going to kill me and the children."

"Shoot her, man," Blake said. "Kill her and we can grab the necklace and run. I've already got a buyer who's going to take it off my hands. Shoot her," Blake said.

Troy fired and hit Blake in his lower leg. Blake screamed in pain and fell to the floor. "Why did you do that, man?"

"Eliza, call the police." Troy reached into the closet and grabbed a stretchy blouse off a hanger. He used it to tie Blake's arms behind his back.

"I'm bleeding to death," Blake cried. "I'm going to sue you. You already had me and you shot me for no reason."

"You made me feel imminent danger to myself, right, Eliza?" Troy said.

She nodded. "You had to shoot him to save yourself and me. And who are the authorities going to believe? You and me, or a man who came into my house through a tunnel in the middle of the night?"

"Exactly," Troy replied.

"Get me some bandages or something before I bleed to death," Blake yelled.

"Quit whining," Troy replied. "It's just a damned flesh wound." He looked at Eliza. His gaze held relief and a wealth of what appeared to be love.

"You should have shot him through his cold, black heart," Eliza said emotionally.

"Where are the kids?" Troy asked.

"Downstairs. I'll go to them and call the police." Eliza flew out of the bedroom and down the stairs. Her heart thundered as she raced into the living room and to the secret hideaway.

She opened the door and the kids came into her arms. They were crying and she was crying. Her tears were ones of relief as she soothed theirs.

She had no idea how Troy had managed to find the tunnel. She had no idea what had brought him to her in the nick of time.

All she knew was that they were all safe now. She hugged the two tightly against her, needing their little bodies in her arms.

She dried their tears and assured them that everything was fine and then led them to the kitchen table. Once they were sitting she made the call to the police.

Troy came into the kitchen and the kids ran to his arms. He bent down and grabbed them to his chest. "It's okay," he said as he hugged them tight. "We're all okay now." He released them and then walked over to Eliza.

He took her by the chin and looked at the wound on the side of her forehead. "Are you sure you're okay? Do you need to go to the emergency room?"

Now that things had calmed down she realized her head hurt, but the pain was manageable. "No, I'm fine," she assured him.

"Let's get this cleaned up." He led her to the sink, where he got a clean cloth out of the drawer and then ran it under warm water so he could wash away the blood.

"Daddy hurt me. I think he's a bad man," Katie said indignantly. "I liked it better when he was in heaven."

"He'll be in prison for a very long time," Troy said softly. His touch was gentle as he moved the cloth against her skin. She closed her eyes for a long moment, grateful that she was the only one who had been wounded, grateful that they were all alive and fine.

"How did you know? How did you know about the tunnel?" she asked.

"I was sitting at my kitchen table doing some soul-searching when I saw the two men run to the wooded area in my backyard. I saw them and then they disappeared. I decided to investigate and here we are." He wiped her forehead one more time and then placed the towel in the sink. "That's better," he said.

At that moment a knock on the door announced the arrival of the police. For the next several hours she and Troy answered question after question and explained about the jeweled necklace Blake had wanted.

The police were shocked by the tunnel and after several of them checked it out they learned that if Troy had taken the other passageway he would have been led to a dead end. Thank God he had chosen the right path. If he'd been just a few minutes longer in arriving, Eliza and her children would have been dead.

Eliza was thankful that Sammy and Katie fell asleep on the sofa before their father was taken out of the house in handcuffs and Mitchell's body was removed.

She had no idea what emotional wounds this night had left behind in her two children. Hopefully none, and if there were some problems with the two dealing with this night of surprise and terror, then Eliza would make sure they got the help they needed.

When the police questioned her about the necklace she told them that her daughter had apparently found it and put it around one of her dolls' necks.

"When did she find it?" Troy asked, obviously surprised by this information.

"I didn't get a chance to ask her," she replied.

"Do you know the doll she's talking about?" Officer Dean Graham, one of the investigating cops, asked her.

Eliza nodded. "I'll go get it." She rose from the kitchen table where they had all been sitting and headed for the stairs. She was grateful that the men working the crime scene had been surprisingly quiet as if in deference to the sleeping children.

She still hadn't really had time to process everything that had happened. In a million years she never would have guessed that not only was Blake still alive, but he'd also been behind the things that had happened in the house.

She supposed she and the kids would go to a motel once the police were finished with her. She didn't have any idea how long the house would be tied up as a crime scene.

She entered Katie's room and saw her four dolls at the little table. Isabella had long red curls and Eliza gasped as she saw the necklace around her neck.

It was stunning, with diamonds that were bigger than any Eliza had ever seen in her life. Even though it had to be dirty after all these years, it shone with a rich luster.

How had Eliza missed it? In all the times she'd seen the doll how could she have missed the fact that the doll wore such a priceless necklace?

Of course, Katie had lots and lots of fake jewelry for her dolls. Eliza didn't always pay attention to what the dolls had hanging around their necks.

She grabbed the doll and hurried back down the stairs. When she reached the kitchen she placed the doll in the middle of the kitchen table.

"I don't want to touch it," she said. "That's what Blake was willing to kill me and his children to possess. I just want it out of here as soon as possible." It was beautiful, but it had been the source of too much terror.

"I imagine there's probably a pretty good reward tied to the return of this," Officer Graham said as he bagged it into evidence.

"I don't want a reward. I just want it out of my possession and back to where it belongs," she replied wearily.

The night had seemed endless and now that the terror of it all was gone, she was left only with exhaustion, a headache and the heartbreak of loving Troy.

He'd run to their rescue, but that didn't mean anything. It didn't mean he suddenly loved her and that he wanted a real relationship with her. It just meant he knew they were in trouble and had run to help.

She would forever be grateful to him. He'd not only saved her life, but more importantly he'd saved Sammy and Katie. Without his intervention there was no doubt that they would have all been killed.

He sat next to her at the table, sober and sharp-eyed as he answered the last of the questions. When all the questions had been asked and answered for what seemed like a hundred times, the officers informed her she needed to find another place to stay for a day or two.

"I'll walk you up so you can pack an overnight bag for you and your children," Officer Graham said to her.

Minutes later she reentered her bedroom. There were several officers in her closet where the door to the tunnel remained open.

It didn't take her long to pack a bag for herself and then she went into Katie's room, where somebody she hadn't seen come into the house was taking pictures of the hidey-holes there.

She packed little bags for each of the kids, adding the Sue Ellen doll in Katie's bag and a handful of miniature cars into Sammy's. She had no idea if Isabella would ever be returned to them.

She'd check them into the nearest motel room and hopefully the children wouldn't be too traumatized by everything that had happened.

Officer Graham helped carry the bags downstairs to the kitchen where Troy stood waiting for her. "Instead of going to a motel, why don't you all come to my house?"

"Oh, I don't think…" she began.

"Please, Eliza. Besides, the kids will feel better about being at my house instead of a strange motel. At least they've stayed at my place before."

It would kill her to be around him knowing he didn't love her the way she wanted to be loved. But she couldn't think about her own mental health right now. He was right about Sammy and Katie. They would feel better staying with Mr. Troy instead of in a motel room.

"Okay," she finally said, far too exhausted to argue even if she wanted to.

Minutes later Officer Graham carried her bags and she carried Katie. Sammy was in Troy's arms as they made their way from her house to his.

"Mommy, what are we doing?" Katie asked sleepily.

"We're going to Mr. Troy's to spend the night," Eliza replied.

"Another slumber party and I'm too sleepy to stay

awake. I'll be mad about this when I wake up," she said. She immediately fell back asleep.

Eliza didn't care how mad Katie got. She was just grateful the little girl was upset about a slumber party instead of being afraid and talking about the night's events.

Someday Eliza would probably have to explain about Blake. She'd have to tell the children that their father had been a bad man. But hopefully the whole truth about Blake wouldn't have to come out for years.

The officer dropped the bags in Troy's foyer and then said he or somebody else might be in touch if any more questions came up. They would try to get the house back in Eliza's possession as quickly as possible. And then he was gone.

Without any conversation they carried the children up to the bedroom where they had spent the night the last time. Once they were tucked in, Eliza followed Troy back down the stairs to retrieve her bag.

Before she could get it, Troy grabbed her arm. "Eliza, I need to talk to you."

She frowned. "I'm really tired, Troy. Whatever it is, can't it wait until morning?"

"No, it really can't wait." He looked troubled. His eyes appeared a darker blue and a knot of tension pulsed in his jawline. "I really need to talk to you before the kids get up."

What now, she thought. After all they'd been through what could he possibly want to discuss now? "Okay," she finally relented.

"How about we go into the kitchen and I'll make some coffee?"

Some of her exhaustion disappeared as she sensed a desperation emanating from him. What in the heck was going on with him? Was he having some sort of post-traumatic stress about shooting Blake? Did this have to do with the anniversary of Annie's death? Did he suddenly feel the need to talk to somebody… anybody? "Coffee sounds good," she agreed.

Minutes later they sat across from each other at the table. "I was sitting right here when I saw the two men run across my yard," he said, finally breaking the silence between them.

She glanced toward his backyard, where several officers were in the wooded area where she now knew a door opened to the tunnel. A sudden shiver ran up her spine. "Thank God you saw them and decided to investigate, otherwise I wouldn't be here drinking coffee with you."

"Before I saw them I had been sitting here soul-searching." He looked down into his cup and then gazed at her once again. She couldn't read his expression, but something about it made her heart beat faster.

"Annie was heavy on my mind, but instead of remembering her death, I remembered her life. Memories of her laughter, of our laughter and love, filled me. And in those memories, I realized Annie wouldn't have wanted me to live my life with only my self-loathing to keep me company. She always loved my happy face, and I want my happy face back."

"That's good, Troy," Eliza said. "I'm so glad if you found some inner peace." She was happy for him if he'd found the forgiveness he'd needed to find for himself to make him whole.

"There's more." He searched her face intently, as if he'd never really seen her before this moment.

"More?" Once again her heart began to beat an unsteady rhythm.

"A wise little girl told me something yesterday. She said she thought God had brought us together because I was a daddy without a daughter and she was a daughter without a daddy. Blake will never be in your children's lives. He'll be in prison for the rest of his life. But Eliza, I want to be the man in Sammy and Katie's life."

He leaned forward, the desperation back in his eyes. "Tell me it isn't too late, Eliza. Tell me you forgive me for being an ass with you. Please tell me you still want me in your life forever, because I can't imagine being anyplace else." His voice trembled and he reached across the table and took her hand in his.

"I love you, Eliza. I love you more than I've ever loved anyone in my life. I pushed you away because I was afraid of how I felt about you. I'd convinced myself that I didn't deserve you, but I do deserve love and happiness in my life. What happened to Annie was a tragedy, but it wasn't a tragedy of my making." He squeezed her hand. "Please tell me you still want to be with me forever."

For a moment her emotions ran so high she couldn't speak. A tremendous joy filled her. "For God's sake please say something," he continued. "If you want me to get down on my knees and grovel, I will."

"That might be fun for me to watch," she said, finally finding her voice. "But you don't need to do that. Troy, I love you as much today as I did yesterday. I want you to be in my life forever. I've never loved a man as much as I love you."

He got up from the table and pulled her up and into his arms. "I want to slumber party with you and the kids every night for the rest of my life," he said, and then his lips captured hers.

The gentle kiss tasted of desire and love and a lifetime of commitment. It was…he was the fairytale ending, the happily-ever-after she'd desired. He would be the father she'd wanted for her children, and together they would have laughter and love.

Epilogue

Troy stood in his backyard and watched the backhoe that was destroying the tunnel and filling it in with dirt. It had been five days since Eliza had welcomed him back into her life, and in those five days a lot of things had been decided.

He was going to put his house on the market and they would live in Eliza's house. Sammy was already adjusted to the space and Troy didn't want to add any stress to the kids by trying to move them.

Besides, his place was market-ready and hers needed a lot of work. He was looking forward to putting in that work and making her house into the best home it could possibly be.

His first order of business had been collapsing the tunnel and filling it in. They would never be vulnerable to somebody sneaking into their house again.

The last five days had been some of the best days

in his entire life. He hadn't realized what a gift he would receive when he fully opened himself up to receiving the love Eliza and the kids gave to him.

He would always remember the daughter he had lost and there would always be sorrow for her loss, but he truly believed Annie would want him to have a happy face, and Eliza and the kids had given that back to him.

He knew deep within his heart that Annie would have approved of him being where he was now. She would have loved him being a father to two children who had really never had one. Annie had been generous that way, and he considered it a tribute to her life that he was now in Sammy's and Katie's lives full-time.

The jewelry store that was the proper owner of the necklace had wanted to give Eliza a $200,000 reward. She had declined it, but they had insisted. She'd finally agreed to accept the reward as long as it was donated to Sammy's school for the blind. He'd been proud of her decision.

There was only one thing he would never, could never talk to Eliza about, and that was the murder pact he'd entered when he'd been out of his mind with grief and rage. He wasn't sorry that Dwight Weatherby had been murdered, and he would own that. But like Nick Simon, all he wanted now was to forget that particular horrible part of his past and focus on his future.

And it was such a bright and wonderful future. He now looked forward to waking up in the mornings with Eliza in his arms. He enjoyed getting up every morning and having breakfast with the kids before they went to school. And he loved coming home to them each day after work.

At five o'clock he motioned to the men to knock off work. "We'll start again in the morning around eight." When the men left he walked across the yard to walk into the front door where he now belonged.

His heart swelled as he reached the kitchen, where Eliza was in the process of getting ready to serve the evening meal. She stood at the stove and he walked up behind her and wrapped her in his arms. He pressed his lips against the side of her neck as her wonderful scent surrounded him.

"Hmm, better hurry with that, my boyfriend will be home any minute," she said.

He laughed and she whirled around in his arms to face him. That smile…he knew he would never get tired of that glorious smile of hers. "How's your day going?" he asked.

"Perfect. I spent the day working on the romance author's website. So, is the tunnel now gone?"

"Almost. The last of it should be gone by noon tomorrow."

"Good." Her eyes darkened a bit and he knew she was remembering the terror.

"Hey, we're good. The bad guys are gone and it's just you and me and the kids." He was glad to see the return of her smile. "By the way, where are the kids?"

"Upstairs playing in Sammy's room. Before I call them down for supper I wanted to tell you something."

He dropped his arms from around her and frowned. "Problems?"

"No, not at all, but a little while ago Katie and Sammy came downstairs to ask me a question. They said since we're slumber partying with you forever now, they wondered if they could call you Daddy Troy."

His chest swelled and tears suddenly misted his eyes. He hadn't expected this…this beautiful gift from her kids…from their kids. "Troy?" She laid her hand on his arm. "If you would prefer they not, it's perfectly okay."

He shook his head. "No… I want that. I'm humbled and honored. I want to be their daddy." He took her into an embrace. "I want them and I want you for the rest of my life." He kissed her with a new joy dancing in his veins and with his heart full of love.

* * * * *

Don't miss Nick Simon's story,
Desperate Strangers,
Available now from Harlequin Intrigue!

INTRIGUE

Available February 19, 2019

#1839 HOSTAGE AT HAWK'S LANDING
Badge of Justice • by Rita Herron
Dexter Hawk's search for the truth about his father's death leads him to a homeless shelter where Melissa Gentry, the love of his life, works. Together, can they stop a dangerous conspiracy that has caused the disappearance of several transients in the area?

#1840 THE DARK WOODS
A Winchester, Tennessee Thriller • by Debra Webb
Sasha Lenoir has always wondered what happened on the night her parents died. Now she'll do anything to learn the truth, even if that means employing the help of US Marshal Branch Holloway—the father of the child she's kept secret for more than a dozen years.

#1841 TRUSTING THE SHERIFF
by Janice Kay Johnson
Detective Abby Baker can't remember anything from the past week. She just knows that someone tried to kill her. Placed under Sheriff Caleb Tanner's protection, can Abby recall what happened before her attacker strikes again?

#1842 STORM WARNING
by Michele Hauf
When a woman is killed, police chief Jason Cash wonders if the killer attacked the wrong person, since Yvette LaSalle, a mysterious foreigner with the same first name as the victim, seems to be hiding in the remote town. Can Jason protect Yvette from an unknown enemy?

#1843 UNDERCOVER PREGNANCY
by Alice Sharpe
Following a helicopter crash, Chelsea Pierce remembers nothing—not even the fact that Adam Parish, the man who saved her, is the father of her unborn child. With determined killers closing in, will Adam and Chelsea be able to save themselves...and their baby?

#1844 THE GIRL WHO COULDN'T FORGET
by Cassie Miles
Twelve years ago, Brooke Josephson and five other girls were kidnapped. Now Brooke and FBI special agent Justin Sloan must discover why Brooke's friend, another former captive, was murdered. Could the psychopath from her childhood be back and ready to finish what he started?

Get 4 FREE REWARDS!

We'll send you 2 FREE Books plus 2 FREE Mystery Gifts.

Harlequin Intrigue® books feature heroes and heroines that confront and survive danger while finding themselves irresistibly drawn to one another.

FREE Value Over **$20**

---

*Looking for his long-lost father reunites cowboy
Dexter Hawk with the only woman he's ever loved.
But can he protect Melissa Gentry when a killer
makes her his next target?*

Read on for a sneak peek at Hostage at Hawk's Landing
from USA TODAY *bestselling author Rita Herron.*

He knew she was shaken, but he wasn't ready to let her out of his sight. "Melissa, you could have been hurt tonight." Killed, but he couldn't allow himself to voice that awful thought aloud. "I'll see that you get home safely, so don't argue."

Melissa rubbed a hand over her eyes. She was obviously so exhausted she simply nodded and slipped from his SUV. Just as he thought, the beat-up minivan belonged to her.

She jammed her key in the ignition, the engine taking three tries to sputter to life.

Anger that she sacrificed so much for others mingled with worry that she might have died doing just that.

She deserved so much better. To have diamonds and pearls. At least a car that didn't look as if it had been rolled twice.

He glanced back at the shelter before he pulled from the parking lot. Melissa was no doubt worried about the men she'd had to move tonight. But worry for her raged through him.

He knew good and damn well that many of the men who ended up in shelters had simply fallen on hard times and needed a hand. But others…the drug addicts, mentally ill and criminals…

He didn't like the fact that Melissa put herself in danger by trying to help them. Tonight's incident proved the facility wasn't secure.

The thought of losing her bothered him more than he wanted to admit as he followed her through the streets of Austin. His gut tightened when she veered into an area consisting of transitional homes. A couple had been remodeled, but most looked as if they